NICK CARTER IS IT!

"Nick Carter out-Bonds James Bond."
—*Buffalo Evening News*

"Nick Carter is America's #1 espionage agent."
—*Variety*

Nick Carter is razor-sharp suspense."
—*King Features*

"Nick Carter is extraordinarily big."
—*Bestsellers*

"Nick Carter has attracted an army of addicted readers . . . the books are fast, have plenty of action and just the right degree of sex . . . Nick Carter is the American James Bond, suave, sophisticated, a killer with both the ladies and the enemy."
—*The New York Times*

FROM THE NICK CARTER
KILLMASTER SERIES

AND NEXT THE KING
CHECKMATE IN RIO
THE DAY OF THE DINGO
DOOMSDAY SPORE
EIGHTH CARD STUD
THE GALLAGHER PLOT
THE JUDAS SPY
THE MAN WHO SOLD DEATH
THE NICHOVEV PLOT
PAMPLONA
THE PEMEX CHART
THE REDOLMO AFFAIR
THE SATAN TRAP
THE SIGN OF THE PRAYER SHAWL
STRIKE OF THE HAWK
TARANTULA STRIKE
TEMPLE OF FEAR
TEN TIMES DYNAMITE
THUNDERSTRIKE IN SYRIA
TIME CLOCK OF DEATH
TRIPLE CROSS
UNDER THE WALL
THE WEAPON OF NIGHT

A Killmaster Spy Chiller

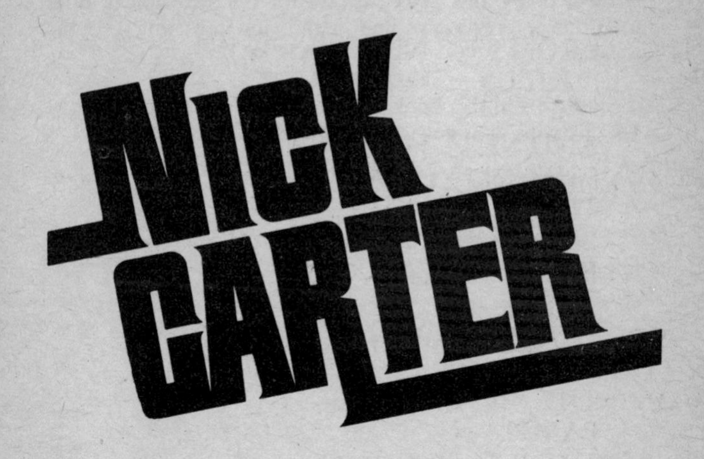

SUICIDE SEAT

A Division of Charter Communications Inc.
A GROSSET & DUNLAP COMPANY
51 Madison Avenue
New York, New York 10010

SUICIDE SEAT

A Charter Original.

First Charter Printing September 1980
Published simultaneously in Canada
Manufactured in the United States of America

2 4 6 8 0 9 7 5 3 1

SUICIDE SEAT

ONE

"You're not Gonzales," the woman said.

"Damn right I'm not," I said.

She backed against the wall, looking at me. She didn't try to reach for anything. I looked her up and down, and she wouldn't have looked bad in that blue robe, with her blonde hair and big blue eyes, if one of those eyes hadn't had a big blue mouse underneath it. As she half-turned I could see other bruises, at the corner of her jaw. "Who are you?" she said. "What do you—?"

"Lady, I admire the spirit," I said. "Most women would have brought the house down on me by now. I'm Nick Carter. I'm here to take you home."

"Home?" she said. Quick tears sprang into her eyes. "H-home? To . . . across the border?"

It was as if she couldn't easily imagine such a thing anymore. I looked hard at her again. In the two or three seconds since I'd mentioned going home, all the tough-broad veneer had dropped off. She suddenly got ten or fifteen years younger, and

I could see now that despite a recent period of hard use and rough living she was the twenty-two-year-old I was looking for after all.

"To the States," I said. "Back to your old man. But get dressed quick. We don't have much time. We're going to have to steal a car as it is." I closed the window behind me.

"Steal a car?" she said. "But . . . but Gonzales is gone. He took the Buick. He—"

"I thought of that," I said. "Get dressed. Please." I listened for sounds of them outside. She went over to a closet and opened the door, poking around inside. "As for cars, there's the one the *burros* were going to drive over the border."

"Oh," she said listlessly. Then, stepping out of the robe, she did a double-take and stood there, naked, looking at me, one hand holding the robe. "But Mr. Carter. The car. It's taped full of—"

"Full of smack," I said, looking at her. She wasn't really the erotic sight you might have expected, pretty as she was. She was all over bruises, and unless you were a dumper or a rough-trade type your eye wouldn't go to the skin, it would go to the bruises. Well, hopefully she'd be saying goodbye to that kind of life in a few minutes.

"Please, Connie. I like the show but time's a-wasting. Get dressed."

She blushed and stepped back inside the closet. "I'm sorry," she said. "I . . . I can't get used to the idea that I might be . . . be free. At last."

"Well, we'll see about that," I said. "The next few hours—maybe the next fifty minutes or so if we're lucky—will tell. First I need to know whether that back road is functional?"

"The one that leads out from the sheds? The garages?"

"Yeah. Does it go through?"

"In good weather," she said. "The rains two days ago may have washed it out in two places. There's a ford in the rainy season. But if you're going to take the four-wheel drive car. . . ."

"Yesh," I said. It made sense to use the convoy car, the one that ran the stuff over the border. Those big oversized tires would hold a hell of a lot of nice brown Sinaloa heroin, taped in neat little waxed-paper packages to the insides of the tires. Or an equal amount of choice Long Pot stuff from Southeast Asia, which would be even more profitable and four to five times as deadly, even cut four times or more. Well, I didn't care which. It wasn't my bag anyhow. My bag was getting the daughter of one of Senator Mike Lovett's most powerful constituents up out of the Baja California hideaway she'd been stashed in for a year and a half now. Once Connie Quitman's little Mexican adventure had ended once and for all, I didn't give a damn if all the H in the world got blown to hell and back.

That sort of stuff was for the drug boys to handle. Me, I was Nick Carter, Killmaster—Agent N3 of AXE, the U.S. Government's little Department of Dirty Tricks.

Well, that's who I thought I was anyhow. . . .

Dressed, she went right back to looking like the cheap slut they'd tried to turn her into. It was the clothes. Gonzales and the other boys he worked with, and loaned her out to, and sometimes even sold her to when somebody was willing to pay him her price—well, they weren't Fernando Lamas or Ricardo Montalban, the kind of Latino whose culture and taste might have preferred her to look like the rich man's lovely daughter that she was. They were border scum: they liked women to look cheap, and they'd dressed her cheap. She looked like the sort of chickie who does sideshows on the little side streets off Revoluçion Avenue in Tijuana —and, thinking this, I reminded myself not to ask her if they'd pressed her into that kind of service too. There was a lot about the present run that I didn't care to know too much about. It would just have made me mad, and I couldn't afford to get mad in my line of work.

"Well," I said now. "There are two of them down there that I know of. The one called Estrada and the one with the scar."

"Cabrera?"

"Yeah, I think so. That sounded more or less like what the other guy called him. Is there anybody else?"

"Only the guard at the garage. But he's trouble. He's a tough one. He's very fast with a gun and even faster with a knife."

"I see. Just plain folks. Okay. We'll take 'em as they come. Can you get the first two up here? Maybe one at a time?"

"Perhaps. Cabrera has been sniffing around me lately but Gonzales has so far kept him off. Maybe I could decoy him."

"Do it," I said. "If we can get the two house guards quietly it might buy me some time to sneak up on the garage man."

"All right," she said. She stepped out into the

hall. "*Paco,*" she said softly. "*Paquito. Estoy solo y triste. Paquito mio. Ven a mi, Paquito mi corazon.*"

Her voice was as mocking as her words—but it was sexy as hell. She knew her man, I was thinking. He said something I couldn't hear, and then I heard his footsteps on the stairs, I stowed Wilhelmina away—that's my vintage Luger with all the original parts—and reached inside my sleeve for another little friend of mine. I call him Hugo, and he's long and slender and pointed and razor-sharp all along the edge, and he makes a lot less noise than Wilhelmina does.

"*Aqui, Paquito,*" she was saying, backing into the door. Then, as she came into sight, I saw her eyes widen. "*Y tu, Manolo? No quiero los dos de vosotros. Por favor, Manolito, ten la bondad de esperar . . . .*" Damnation! Her little call had brought both of them! And despite what she was saying, the second one, Manolo, wasn't about to wait.

She backed into the doorway all the way now, and a hand snaked out and grabbed her arm as she did.

Hugo went into his arm halfway between wrist and elbow. He slid in like a hot razor into butter—and twisted. Paco groaned and let go. I swung Hugo around and cut his throat with one sweep. He staggered forward. I gave him a shove and dove for the other one. Manolo had a gun halfway out when I reached him. I let him have a swipe of Hugo across the gun-hand's wrist and, with the other hand, drove a straight left into his kisser. He tumbled over the guardrail backward and fell maybe ten feet to the landing. I looked down at him; his head was still attached to his body, but at a crazy sort of angle. I turned back to the upstairs room.

She was standing looking down at the other one. There was no pity in her eyes. The pool of red spread out from his ruined neck. He had perhaps a moment or two left.

"Let's go," I said, and, taking no chances, I retrieved the guns both of them had been toting and handed one to the girl. The other I stuffed in my belt. It was still fifty miles to the border.

She stopped at the stairs and took off her stilt-heeled shoes.

"I can't even walk in these things," she said, "much less run."

She led the way down the stairs, but let me take the lead after that. At the back door she stopped me.

"Look. Calderon—the guard at the garage—he's very good with guns. He is also a—a *maricon.* He is more interested in boys than he is in the likes of me. I can't decoy him."

"Not even by hollering bloody murder?"

"Probably not. He isn't even turned on by the idea of hurting women. He's just plain indifferent. We don't exist."

"Okay," I said. "Can you drive? And are the keys likely to still be in the car?"

"I can drive," she said. "It's a Jeep. Stolen from the American Army. They don't have keys, just turn-on switches."

"You lie low until I holler for you," I said. "I'm going in after him."

I winked at her and stepped out into the yard. *"Hola, pajarito!"* I bellowed. *"Calderon! Donde esta mi bugaron favorito, el mamalon mas favorito de todo el mundo?"* If that wouldn't rouse him, I was thinking, I didn't know what would. I had just called him a fairy, a bugger, and the world's champion cocksucker in a total of three sentences.

He stepped out into view—and dove for his gun. He was fast as hell.

I was faster. Wilhelmina must have liked him. She fairly jumped into my hand. I got him in the shoulder and he went down. He rolled when he hit. Two rolls, and the gun was in his other hand, and he squeezed off a round that damn near parted my hair for me.

"Nick!" the girl's voice said. "Someone's coming! It's Gonzales—and the others!"

There wasn't time to duck for cover. I fired point-blank and caught him in the middle of the forehead. "Come on!" I yelled. "Make for the garage!"

Running barefoot, she got there nearly as fast as I did. "I'll drive," I said. "Here." I threw her the second gun. "They'll probably take off after us. Keep 'em busy. Just fire at 'em. I don't care if you don't hit anyone, although I won't get mad at you if you do. Just keep 'em ducking." I jumped into the seat beside her and fired up the car. The engine roared—and that wasn't any wheezy old Jeep engine under that sawed-off hood, let me tell you. "Hang on," I said, and took off in a racing start. The car hit two bumps and bounced. We both went up in the air, off the seats, and came down hard, but when we came down we were barreling along at a hell of a clip and I was speed-shifting. That wasn't any sluggish old Jeep transmission either.

"They're coming behind us," she said. She turned around in the seat and fired once, twice.

"Okay," I said. "Keep a grip on something.

That Buick is faster than we are, but if I—"

"Don't count on the terrain helping us," she said. "His car has racing shocks. Off-the-road racing shocks."

I'd have to count on our higher clearance helping us out, I was thinking. And then I floored it and to hell with the terrain.

There was a rise up ahead, high enough that you couldn't see the road beyond it. I took out after it, bouncing.

We went over the bump two feet in the air, hit and bounced. I braked hard and spun the wheel. She hung on for dear life beside me. The Jeep came to a dead stop in the middle of the road—facing the way we'd come. We were blocking the hell out of that two-rut road. Looking them right in the eye. I turned on my headlights: the bright beams.

"Nick!" she said. "What are you doing?" Her eyes were full of fear—sudden, stark fear.

"Easy does it," I said, grinning. "He'll be along in a sec." And sure enough, the Buick came over the rise like a bat out of hell. And even through the tinted glass you could see the shock and terror on the driver's face as he saw, not a clear road ahead, but the Jeep blocking his entire path. I honked the horn hard, three times.

It was the last straw. He jerked on the wheel, braked. It wasn't enough. The Buick swerved, bounced, hit and bounced again, hit something and flipped high into the air. I saw somebody's body come flying out as the car came down. The car hit the body and mashed it flat; then the car itself came apart on the next bounce, and as the hood and doors flew open something ignited the gas tank and it exploded while it was still in the air.

The explosion was deafening, the cloud black and hot.

Then there was silence. In the summer quiet we could see, far down the dirt road, a wheel, sheared right off in the wreck, spinning and bouncing for many yards across the chaparral before it came to rest.

"Now let's see if we can turn this damn thing around and get the hell out of here."

TWO

Now if this were the U.S.A., the smart thing to do right now would have been to stick to the back roads and avoid the highways and the main drags and all the places where your car could get stopped and searched. Especially since we didn't know how many of our pursuers had gone up in the wreck—or how many might still be laying for us. After all, it wasn't too far to the border, and as long as you retained your sense of direction—you ought to be able to find your way just by heading in the right direction long enough.

But of course it wasn't the United States. It was Baja California, and the good roads there are like the bad roads here. And their bad roads? Forget it. That country is wild. There are still cannibal tribes down there, and even Spanish disappears not too far from the main highway. And English? What's that?

So it was back to the main road and that was that. We bounced along at a reasonable clip and still got our teeth shaken out of our heads. It was a wonder we were able to talk at all.

"Nick," she was saying, "you haven't asked me The Question yet."

"Which one?" I said. And then I figured out what it was. "Oh, yeah. You mean the one about how did a nice girl like you wind up in a place like this?"

"That's the one," she said. I shot her a glance, lousy potholed road or no. Her eyes were dark and angry. "Let me tell you, I"—And then something caught in her throat, and the next thing I knew she was weeping bitterly on the seat beside me, weeping as if she'd lost everything she had.

Well, maybe she almost had. Maybe she had indeed. We still weren't across that border yet.

I stopped the car.

"Hey," I said. "Here. Tell me." She hid her face in my chest and howled like a baby. I let her. All the while running my eyes around us, keeping alert. There was just enough traffic to keep me worried.

The stop was worth it in a way. I think if I hadn't stopped and held her like that she wouldn't have been able to tell me about it. It wasn't the kind of stuff you talk over coffee at a restaurant, you can be damned sure about that.

It's a lousy racket, one of the lousiest. And one of the biggest, and most profitable. And it's the one you never read about in your daily newspaper. The Interpol statistics about international white slavery aren't exactly family reading. "White?" Well, the term doesn't mean much. The people in charge aren't picky. They'll enslave any female they can get. It doesn't matter who she is and what she looks like, as long as she can be sold to some guy for hard cash. And the outcome of it all sure as hell isn't liberation.

It's not all the papers' fault. At Interpol's 34th international session of chiefs of police in 1965 the subject for the conference was "international traffic in women under cover of employment exposing them to prostitution." After a period of study a panel made recommendations, which were unanimously adopted by the police body. They called for international agreements and police cooperation.

What happened? The recommendations were never released to the press or the public. Why? "Some governments might be embarrassed."

In 1966 the whole subject was swept under the table in an UNESCO meeting: according to the Soviet delegate and the African bloc—the latter group had a lot to hide, it later appeared—"apartheid, racism and colonialism were more pressing problems, and only these should be regarded as manifestations of modern slavery." The matter was tabled. Why? As the Russian delegate said, "governments were perfectly capable of dealing with problems such as slavery themselves."

Sure they were.

Connie Quitman's story wasn't anything special. It sounded like a lot of others I'd heard—most of them involving the Middle East or the African continent or South America or the Far East instead of Mexico, but all of them working some variety of the same old scam.

Here's how it works:

The girl finds herself in a tailspin. She's had a bad love affair. Or she's had a spat with her parents. Or she's flunking out of school and—but you know the story. We had a damn nation of runaways for ten years or so and they all had some variety or other of the same kind of story to tell.

Then the classified section of the newspaper waves this "golden opportunity" under her nose. Sometimes the scam is a job with a "ballet" company, no experience needed. Sometimes it involves traveling as "secretary" to an important businessman, duties not spelled out. Sometimes it involves "supervised travel" with the company to glamorous places. All expenses paid, of course, even during the training period. Qualifications: a nice lively personality, neatness, a passport.

Once you're out of the U.S. and in the proper jurisdiction where the cops have been paid off at the top, they lower the bridge on you. You wind up getting drugged, drunk or doped. They throw you into the middle of an orgy and then shoot pictures of your antics. When you wake up they show you the Polaroids and tell you how much the folks back home—the folks you'd otherwise count on to try to bail you out of this—would enjoy seeing the pix. You look at the snapshots, and there you are servicing three people at a time, this doped-up grin on your face.

And from there it just gets worse. And in most of those countries there's nobody to talk to about it. Somebody trying to help you, in certain Middle Eastern countries, can get run out of the country overnight for trying to rock the boat. In some African countries he can wind up in jail on an indefinite hitch. In other African countries he can wind up dead. And you? You're expendable.

Connie's story hadn't been much different than

anyone else's. In her case the difference was having a father who knew a Senator. And in having been sold within fifty miles of the U.S. border. That ought to have made it easy to get away.

"Nick," she said. "I . . . I'm sorry. I just . . ."

"That's okay, Connie," I said. "You gotta get it out somehow. I understand. But now—"

"You're right," she said, sitting up. "The main thing is getting out. But how? How are we—?"

"I've been thinking about that," I said. "Let me tell you, I'm not nuts about riding around in this damn thing. Not when the tires are all full of horse. Not when they know the car and will report it. Not when, in all likelihood, the cops down here are part of the operation."

"Yes," she said. "I know that somebody on the force is. Somebody fairly high up. Gonzales had him on the payroll. You know about the *mordida?*"

"Yeah. The 'bite.' You don't have any idea who?"

"No. Except that Gonzales never deals with—never dealt with anybody petty if he could help it. Nick, whoever it is, I wouldn't know him by sight, perhaps, but I might recognize his voice."

"Why?"

"They . . . rented me out to him one night. It was dark. I never saw his face. But I would know his voice. And his wrist—there was a scar on it. It was a long welt from a knife wound. It was in the shape of a cross. Nick, let's go. I'm getting scared again. Just thinking . . . ."

"Yeah." I hit the starter. "I know what you mean." I didn't. No man could, I guess. But I could make a guess or two, I sure as hell didn't want her to have to live through that again.

And you can imagine: she'd tried to escape. That would make anything they'd done to her before, breaking her in after they'd conned her into taking that "secretarial" gig in Mazatlan, look tame. And that first time she'd been raped twenty times in one night . . . . Well, that's enough details. You want any more S and M stuff, go to your nearest adult book store for it. And try to avoid me when you come out. I don't want to see you.

The road sort of muddles along through most of the way past one grubby coastal town after another, and in between each pair of grubby coastal towns, these days, is a rich fourflusher's condo development for the rich Americans with their coupons and their investments and their pork belly futures and their goddam whatever. Why the border Mexican stays as good-natured, decent and polite as he does I don't know. Unless he has ideas about migrating over the border sans green card or passport, and just doesn't feel like making any waves. Meanwhile, the coast part, the part nature put in before the horse's ass developers took over, is breathtakingly pretty. We don't have anything like that up the coast on our side of the frontier, not for many miles, not until you start getting into the Hearst country up above San Luis Obispo.

We hadn't a care in the world, tooling along like that, until the damn rear tire blew. And what the hell chose to come bearing down on us just then but one of the courtesy cars the Mexican government is putting on the roads down there right now, to improve the friendly relations between our nice rich country and theirs in the wake of the opening of that nice new toll road down to Cabo San Lucas.

"Hello, *Señor,*" the cop said, stepping out of the car. "May I help you with this?" All smiles.

I shot her a glance. No, thanks, the last thing in the world I wanted right now was a cop helping me change a tire with the damn tires all stuffed full of white powder. "*Mil gracias, Señor,*" I said, backpedaling madly, "*pero no—*"

"But no," he said politely. "Please. You must let me." He smiled a friendly gold-toothed smile. He was looking me up and down—and her too. Sizing us up. We didn't fit somehow.

Suddenly the bitch box went on in his car. He went over to answer it, excusing himself.

"Señor," said the cop when he came back, "May I trouble you for your license? And the registration of this automobile?"There has been a report, there was a . . . an incident south of here. All cars are being stopped for questioning." His English was perfect. His manner was just right. I had the feeling he was a good cop. "Your registration, please?" he said again.

"I don't have it," I said. "The car was borrowed from a friend. Look, if you like we can—"

"I'm afraid I'll have to ask you to come with me," he said. "You and the lady. You—" He looked up for a moment, behind me, down the road. As I looked around to where his eyes had gone I saw a Mexican Army deuce-and-a-half bearing down on us, with a squad of machine-gun-toting *Federales* on the back. It screeched to a halt not ten feet from the Jeep and the officer in charge was out of the door and down to the ground no more than a split-second later. He was a dark *indio* type, sturdily built, all business. Except for his eyes.

There was something more in them: trouble, gratuitous trouble, the kind I didn't need at all.

"*Mi coronel,*" said the cop, saluting.

"*Teniente,*" said the officer. Behind him the squad jumped down from the truck, automatic weapons at the ready. "*Qué tal aquí?*"

Connie's fingers suddenly dug into my arm. I looked at her. Her face was white with shock. Her eyes stared blindly.

I looked at the officer's wrist. There was a livid scar on it, a scar in the shape of a cross.

THREE

I looked him up and down. I didn't find a weak spot anywhere. He was in his forties, his hair was still squeaky Indian black, as was the downcurling black mustache.

"You," he said in English. "Where did you get this Jeep?"

"I borrowed it," I said.

"You stole it."

"That's ridiculous," I said. "Who claims I stole it?"

He looked at Connie just once, dismissed her, and looked back at me. It'd been dark for him too, that night he'd been casually handed a woman to rape, the way you'd hand somebody a *porrón* full of red wine. "I say you stole it. You will come with me."

"Okay," I said, shrugging. "Whatever you say." Mexico is Napoleonic Code, not British Common Law. There's no presumption of innocence. I turned to the courtesy-car cop. "The lady . . . could you give her a lift into town? She was just hitching a ride." Before he could nod, I turned to her. *"Lo siento, Señorita, pero hay que ir con este señor, aquí. Hasta la vista."* I thought about it for a second, and then turned back to the courtesy man. "Could you do me a favor?" I said. "Could you call my lawyer?" I handed him a card. It said *"Armando Segura, Abogado."* It had an address and phone number, Tijuana. He wasn't a lawyer.

The cop took it, looked at me hard, and looked at the colonel. Then he put it in his pocket. "I will call him. Your name?"

"Nick Carter."

"All right. Now I think you will go with the *coronel.*" He nodded courteously in the dark man's direction. He was a good cop.

"Okay," I looked back at her one time. Her eyes were full of fear. But they were also full of hope and determination. And I hadn't seen much of either quality there before. If she could get a ride into Tijuana, I was thinking, she could walk across the border—and into the Chula Vista police station, to call Daddy collect. She tried to smile, a little. It cheered me up. A little.

"Hasta luego," I told her. And turned back to the *coronel* and his *Federales*. I looked him in the eye once. And I didn't like at all what I saw there.

The truck stopped once, just on the other side of town, where the colonel got out and made a pay phone call from a booth. I was sure that he knew about the Jeep! I'd heard him, just before we left, telling the young cop not to touch the car but to leave it where it was. And of course, being in on the deal, he'd known the whole business: the tires full of skag, the whole thing. Everything but the reason I was there. He'd figured out that I was stealing the stash, but he hadn't figured out that it was only incidental and that the main thing I wanted from the damn Jeep was transportation. And he hadn't connected the girl with any of it.

At least she had a fifty-fifty chance.

And me? Well, we'd see.

They took me in the back room the minute we got to the slammer. The first thing the dark *indio* colonel had done, once they'd shoved me into the little room with my hands manacled behind my back, was to kick me in the pills and then, as I doubled over, knee me in the face. That was his warm-up.

A bucket of ice-cold water hit me in the face. I raised my head a little and shook it. Then it sank back down on that hard concrete floor. My hands were still behind my back. Getting up would have been a chore even if I weren't tired to hell and gone.

Coronel Iglesias looked down at me, his face still impassive, Indian style. "Now," he said, "the Jeep? Where were you going? Who was in this with you? Why—?"

Somebody came in the door just then, though. I leaned my bloody cheek on the concrete and watched them talk.

"Mi coronel."

"Si?"

The intruder—he seemed to be a noncom—whispered to Iglesias. The Indian frowned slightly; it was the first sign of emotion I'd seen in him. "*Pues . . . traigalo consigo.*" He gave me a glance of cold contempt and went out, his bootheels clicking on the concrete of the hall floor. The noncom helped me to my feet and into an adjacent room.

Before long, the door swung open and Armando Segura stepped in. He looked back through the glass on the door. Then he searched the little room for bugs. When he'd satisfied himself that there were none he sat down in the chair opposite my bench.

"You look like hell," he said in his flawless, if slightly accented, English.

"Don't ask me how I feel," I said. "It'll only depress you." I looked at him through the one eye left open. He looked even tougher, meaner, and more inscrutable, than Iglesias and I knew that he was. We'd worked together before.

"The young policeman called in," he said. "He is not part of it. He is new, down from the capital. He went to a lecture I gave once at the school where he was trained."

"Good. He's a good cop."

"Yes now, what do we do about you?"

"You know that Jeep's tires are full of horse. Iglesias is in on the deal. He was on the take. They were going to smuggle the shit over the border."

"The Jeep's gone."

"He works quick," I said.

"He planted a bundle of heroin in your coat as they brought you in. You are being held as a drug smuggler."

"And the girl?"

"The policeman saw her to the border. When he called in to me I told him that he should help her, that you must have known what you were doing. Did you?"

"I thought I did at the time. Now, I'm not so sure. But I'm glad she made it. She was the reason I came over. What the hell do I care about heroin?"

"Okay. Only—your present situation—"

"That's just what I was going to ask you, as my 'lawyer.' Where the hell do I stand?"

"Up to your nostrils in quicksand," Segura said. "And sinking fast. You are being framed. To cover Iglesias's little raid on the Jeep."

"Looks like I gotta get through to Washington." I said.

"Nick," Segura said. "I don't think that's possible."

"What the hell are you trying to tell me? You're supposed to be on my side. You . . . ."

"Nick. I *am* on your side."

"But . . . ."

"Do you think Iglesias has been pulling all this off with impunity? *Madre de dios,* man, he's been under surveillance for six months. Maybe more."

"Well, what the hell am I doing in the slam?"

"Nick. The girl is okay. Your job is done. In a moment or two I am going back through that door and we are going to take Iglesias, just you and me and him, on a little ride. I am going to tell him that you have a little confession to make, one which cannot be shared with any of his subordinates. It was the only thing I could do under the circumstances. Anyhow, we're going to tell him you have a line into a big stash of heroin that Gonzales and his friends were holding out on him. Something they had had no intention of paying him his own percentage of. I've already given him some hints of this. And we're going to tell him we know where it is. It's up across the border, where all he has to do is go along with us and then fix it with the border people on the way back over. I want to catch him, Nick, I want to—*como se dice?*—I want to waste him. He is a vulture."

"I understand all that. And I'm glad to help out. I take it you've been in touch with Washington."

"Nick, I've been in touch with Washington—but we're definitely out in the cold on this. I couldn't get through to Hawk. Something's very wrong there. I couldn't get through to anyone who would admit that Hawk, or AXE, or you or me ever existed . . ."

FOUR

"Can you get my damn weapons? And something to pick these damn cuffs with?"

"I can get the weapons. I have a man here in the office. We'll have to leave the cuffs on until we're out of this place. Iglesias must not suspect anything."

"Okay." I straightened my back—and wished I hadn't. Whatever else you could say about the *coronel*, he was no slouch at the business of giving somebody the third degree. "Let's go."

Iglesias took no chances on getting caught. He came along with us alone, and let Segura drive. I was at the stage where all I could do, in those cramped quarters, was sit there and suffer. And wish the Mexican highways were smoother. And wish that Segura's shocks were softer. Me? He'd undone one cuff for a moment and run it through the doorhandle before clipping it back on me again. I was trussed like a pig.

We cut back south on the same rickety old highway, between the toll road and the sea, past the squalid slums that separated T.J. from the ocean, past the Bull Ring by the Sea, past Rosarito.

"Hey," I said. "The deal was that the goods were up across the border."

"Relax," Iglesias said. His eyes on me were cold and deadly. "We are not only going to find them, we are going to bring them back. And we cannot do that by land." He pulled out a long black panatela, cut it, and lit it. "I have a boat down the coast."

I looked at him, then looked up ahead at the road, past Segura's impassive neck and shoulders. I didn't like that too much. . . . But maybe, I reflected, it might work out best in the long run. Iglesias, at sea, would possibly be easier for us to handle.

I didn't think about the things Segura had told me. Time enough for worrying about that once we were in American waters.

"Turn here," Iglesias said suddenly. I looked up ahead. A side road led up over the ridge and back down toward the sea. Iglesias settled back in the seat, his hands in his lap. He'd changed from his colonel's uniform to civvies: a well-cut ice cream suit that somehow made him look even more *indio* than before. Segura slowed, turned, headed up the rocky road slowly.

As we crested the hill we could see a rocky harbor, with a few fishing boats tied up. The tide was coming in. By high tide the waves would be sweeping into those little inlets like nobody's business, sending showers of spray high in the air. Now you could see it pulling on the anchored boats. There was nobody at the landing, nobody at all.

"Park here," Iglesias said. I'll spare you the Spanish from here on. It was all in Spanish. Segura pulled over and turned off the key.

"Out," Iglesias said.

The coast along Baja isn't anything at all like the coast of the Eastern United States. For one thing, that nice shallow Continental Shelf you're used to just isn't there at all. There's a narrow strip of perhaps ten-fathom water that goes out to a mile or two, and then it just drops off. A few miles past Los Coronados, due southwest from T.J., you could lose all your line and never find bottom at all. Down there it's all deep trenches and canyons. It makes a fine playground for the marine biologist.

It also makes a fine grave.

I sat, hands still manacled, and watched Segura at the wheel. What we were going north in, by stages, was a sixty-foot inboard that must have been old enough to have been a sailboat once. There was a little cabin, and we were sitting in it. Iglesias was smoking a cigar. He didn't offer me one.

Out on the blue you could see the dolphins jumping. The sky was bright and clear, and the smell in the air was the fresh smell of salt spray. At the right season, this far out into the darker water, you might find yourself sailing along right smack dab in the middle of a pod of grey whales: big friendly bastards, longer—and stronger—than your boat, and powerful enough to dump you over any time they wanted to.

Now, a little to the north, we could see San Clemente Island looming, and beyond that the even higher profile of Catalina. They looked like Bali Hai and its kid sister.

I was wondering why we hadn't turned north toward the mainland—and wondering where Segura had stashed my weapons. We hadn't had a chance to talk about anything since Iglesias had come back into the interrogation room.

Under our feet the inboard chugged. We bobbed along like a motorized cork on a slowly heaving cushion of three hundred fathoms of blue water.

Off our port bow I could see a shark fin, circling lazily.

"All right," Iglesias said. "Here."

Segura turned, his eyes puzzled. His mouth opened slightly. Then his eyes narrowed as he saw the snubnose .38 Iglesias was pointing at his middle.

"Shut it down," Iglesias said. He wasn't smiling at all. He was the same expressionless *indio.* Only now there was a hard sharp cutting edge on that dead voice of his. Iglesias, nice and businesslike, had thumb-busted the hammer back. "This is the end of the line," he said. "I had been trying to learn who their man was in Tijuana. Now I know."

"Whose man?" Segura said. "Look, are we going after that stash of heroin or aren't we? If you—"

"There isn't any stash of heroin," Iglesias said. "The decoy won't work. You had an idea of getting rid of me. It won't work. Instead I will get rid of you. Did you think I was going to let you break up an operation that was making me rich?"

"Look," I said, "I don't know what you're up to, but—"

"Shut up," Iglesias said.

There'd only be the one moment when I could go after him. The same was true of Segura. If one of us jumped him the other would have the split-second in which the first guy was getting killed to operate in.

I got my feet under me.

"A friend of mine called in," Iglesias told Segura. "This *gabacho*"—he indicated me with a twitch of one shoulder—"killed five of our people. He got away in a Jeep whose tires were full of heroin. We have the Jeep now."

"But there's more," Segura said. "Up the coast—"

"That may be," Iglesias said. "It will no longer be your affair—"

Segura jumped him. With those coal-black eyes wide open: he knew what he was doing. And it came as no surprise to him, I'm sure, when the snubnose gun roared and a heavy slug ripped into his chest, spinning him around.

I didn't even have the time to watch him fall. I was diving at Iglesias, cuffed hands held out in front of me. My shoulder hit him hard and spun him against the wall. The gun went toward the ceiling. It went off, once. And then I swung my cuffed hands, together. The wallop I gave him snapped his head to one side. The gun's barrel faltered.

I kicked him in the balls. The gun went down toward me, but his hand on its handle wasn't in control any more. His face took on an expression of pain, the first expression I'd seen him register at all so far.

He recovered damn fast. The gun swung down and belted me one on the side of the neck, where I was already sore enough as it was. On the upswing it was going to drill me one just the way he'd drilled Segura. I went back on one leg and kicked with the other.

My foot caught his wrist and deflected the gun's path. I recovered quickly and aimed another kick at his face. It caught him on one cheekbone. I could feel his face give, through those steel toe-caps on my shoe. And I swung another two-handed blow at his gun arm.

The revolver hit the deck and scuttled away. And now he had some recovering to do. He came at me.

He wasn't any damn sissy himself. That first rush was a pro lineman's; his shoulder hit me amidships hard and drove me all the way across the little cabin. And now he dug a fist into my ribs, hard enough to bend me over. I came back up with both manacled hands in fists.

But Segura hadn't cut off the ignition. The tiller was going crazy, and so was the boat; we were chugging around in circles. Now we hit a big swell and the unattended tiller swung her around hard. She almost flipped over on one side—and I did a somersault and landed on my ear.

I got up shaking my head. Iglesias was scuttling through the open door toward the gun out on the deck. There wasn't time to race him for it. Instead I grabbed for the tiller, swinging it about hard.

The momentum of it swung the gun away; it slid down the length of the long deck, and Iglesias hit the deck and rolled.

While he was recovering I grabbed for Segura's briefcase. Sure enough, there was my Luger. The familiar knurled handle settled into my fist. I jumped out onto the open deck and tried to draw a bead, with the boat spinning wildly underfoot.

Iglesias had the .38 aimed, and he squeezed off a round. It whistled by my ear. I held my arms out again and shot him between the eyes, just as the boat heeled over and threw me ass over teakettle. My head must have hit something hard.

What probably saved my neck was the fact that the engine seemed to have stalled out. I looked out over the blue Pacific—and saw a boat on the horizon.

I rushed back inside the cabin. There was a pair of 7 x 50 binoculars on a table; I peeled off the lens covers and zeroed in on the vessel. It was a big Coast Guard cutter, flying the American flag—and it was heading my way.

I ditched the glasses and hustled back on deck. I had time to wire a couple of weights to Iglesias's legs and drop him over the side into a three-thousand-foot trench. Then, with more regret, I did the same to Segura. I retrieved Hugo and Pierre and was just putting the finishing touches on a good lock-pick job when the cutter drew up alongside and hailed me.

Me? Sure I'd be glad to hitch a ride. . . .

There were some hassles. What was I doing in U.S. waters in a boat registered in Mexico? That sort of thing. There were some eyebrows lifted over the fresh bullet hole in the cabin. I thought I was settling all the scores, though, when I presented my credentials.

Even a big cutter takes time coming in to port, and by the time the big grey vessel chugged into San Diego Harbor there'd been time to call in and check up on me. I was slurping up good swab-jockey coffee in the galley when the young lieutenant in charge came in, flanked by two hefty seamen.

"Mr. Carter?" he said. "I'm afraid I'll have to ask you to come my way."

They're nicer about it in the Coast Guard than they are even down at the gringo slammer. I not only got a free telephone call to my lawyer, I got as many calls as it took to reach him.

That was damn nice of them, considering the lawyer I was calling was Senator Mike Lovett, in Washington.

An aide finally put him on. "Nick? Good work. I got a call from Bill Quitman an hour ago. The San Diego police are sending her home."

"Great. But Senator. . . ."

"Yeah, I know what you're calling about. Nick, it's out of my hands for now. I can't do a damn thing about it. Not until I can get it read into the Congressional Record, and start bitching about it on the Senate floor. And under the circumstances, I'm getting some pressure from the White House not to do that."

"I don't under—"

"I mean, Nick. I've got a crucial bill of my own that desperately needs Administration support, and if I go rocking the boat now on one of the President's pet—"

"Excuse me," I said. "I'm missing out on something. Something's happened to my security status and I don't know what it is."

"Jesus, you *don't* know, do you? Nick, you know that I was one of the half dozen legislators to know about AXE. And from now on, I never heard of you. It's a new Washington, Nick."

"For the love of God. You're not kidding."

"Nick, that's not the worst of it. The . . . uh . . . admiral put the word out covertly. Stay away from Washington. You're not wanted.

"Oh, come on, Mike. Who do they think they're—"

"Nick, keep in touch somehow. I'll do what I can."

"Yeah." I thanked him and hung up. Only then did I remember I'd originally called him to get some help with the Coast Guard. It took one more call to fix that. But then I was footloose and fancy free.

FIVE

I called Jake Quitman.

"Hello?"

"Jake? This is Nick Carter. I. . . ."

"Nick! Thank God. I just heard. I'm taking off for San Diego to pick her up. You just caught me going out the door. I—what can I say? Good work I—"

"Jake. She's been through a lot. More than she'll ever be able to tell you."

"Nick—"

"Do me a favor."

"Jesus. You name it." Jake was worth perhaps a million and a quarter and rising fast. "You've got a blank check."

"Don't ask her about it."

"But Nick—"

"Don't ask her. You said *you name it,* and I just named it. Don't ask her. Just love her. Love her to damn death. She's grown up fast. She needs to go back to being a kid again for a while, I think. Help her. Both of you help her. She's a good girl."

The article in the New York *Times* didn't mention AXE by name. Hell, virtually no one knew about it. It was probably buried in the budget under something totally innocuous. But the article left no doubt in my mind that Mike had known what he was talking about.

I still wanted to hear it from David Hawk—Hawk, the gruff, cigar-chewing, tough-talking, hard-as-nails chief of AXE. There wasn't a sign of him. Number no longer in operation, no forwarding address.

I called Lovett and learned that the situation looked permanent. In one stroke the most complex network of espionage and intelligence operations in the world—and the most valuable one—had been shattered. It occurred to me to offer my services to MI5; but that would have required two things I didn't want to do at the moment: leaving the U.S. and going underground.

If I was going to find Hawk, the first step was to make myself as visible as possible. To that end, I set myself up in business—the only business I knew.

I took out a license, had four business cards printed, hooked up four phones in a Manhattan office, put ads in the Manhattan yellow pages, and the yellow-pages of the Washington, Chicago, L.A. and Atlanta phone books as well.

I ran a small discreet display ad in the *New York Times Magazine,* listing the firm name that a reader of the *Times Magazine* was most likely to respond to. It read something like this:

T. WOODMAN AND
ASSOCIATES
Discreet Investigations

* Missing Persons
* International Inquiries
* Industrial Work a Specialty

There was a logo in one corner that would be recognized by perhaps a hundred people in the world. It was the symbol for AXE.

It took two weeks before I got the first of the calls I was looking to get. Not work calls. There were six of those before the ink on the Sunday *Times* was dry. I took three of those jobs. Two of them were done in two days, at a net profit of $26,000. The third took another three days. At this rate I was going to get muscle-bound just carrying the money to the bank.

Then that first call came in. The *real* one.

"T. Woodman," I said in my best cold, dead male-secretary voice.

"Cut out the shit, Nick. I'd recognize that voice anywhere."

"I beg your pardon?" I wasn't going to give up without a battle.

"God damn it, you used that one on me in Manila. Once bitten twice shy."

"Dick Potter." I dropped the accent.

"Sounds better than N8, doesn't it? I mean, in this day and age."

"Huh. And you're . . . ah . . . at liberty, as we knights of the road used to say?"

"You are so right. And bored to goddam tears."

"Me too. Want to come fill out an application?"

"Nice long waiting list, huh?"

"Yeah," I lied. "But for you I'll make a special deal. Today only. Tell you what I'm gonna. . . ."

"Be right down," he said. He hung up.

I grinned at the dead phone. It was working, I thought. And damn fast too.

Now for that other ad in the *London Times.* And the other one in *Mainichi Shimbun.* And the one in *La Prensa,* in Buenos Aires. And the ones in Hong Kong, and Manila, and Rio, and Paris, and Rome, and Teheran and Tel Aviv and. . . .

Never mind the language. Translated, they'd all say the same thing.

Ally ally oxen free. . .

SIX

By Christmas I'd signed up, around the world, every one of AXE's operatives up through N22—no, almost every one; N5 was dead and there hadn't been any time to replace him—and all four of my businesses were making money hand over fist.

No, let me qualify that. Three of them were. The fourth phone number was one for folks who couldn't afford us, but who needed us anyhow. I figured the other three were fat enough to give that one a free ride.

Anyhow, there we were with virtually everyone aboard. You ask me how the hell I met that kind of payroll. I didn't. Every one of the ops was working on commission, including me. For one thing, it was a matter of pride. If you'd worked for David Hawk you had a built-in resistance to working for anybody else—including me—as a salaried employee.

For another thing, you made more damn money that way.

It was a nice logical setup. There was no need to screen employees. They'd already been screened by Hawk—the best litmus paper in the world—and I knew all of 'em either by sight or by reputation. Inside of six months or so I had myself the best network of private operatives in the world.

There was only one thing missing.

David Hawk.

He'd literally disappeared from the face of the earth. His mail came back unopened, with a Postal Service stamp on it. His house had been sold. All attempts to put a tracer on him—even attempts by my own network—wound up on dead-end streets.

His name even disappeared from *Who's Who*, where he'd been listed for twenty years as head of the Amalgamated Wire Services, the front organization for AXE. You couldn't find him in the phone book, or the Washington Green Book, or on any document official or unofficial in the United States.

Hell, maybe he'd retired. Lord alone knew he'd been at it long enough. To build up a great organization like that—one that had, in all modesty, saved the peace of the world dozens of times, quietly and undercover—and then have it scuttled in the name of Good Government. . . . Well, maybe I'd have retired too. In disgust. And bought myself a fortress on a mountaintop, with a moat and a Keep Out sign and a dozen fierce dogs.

Meanwhile, most of our work was fairly high-level stuff. A lot of it was industrial espionage or counterespionage. Several of our crowd had good international backgrounds at that sort of thing.

Embezzlements? Missing persons? Fuzzy bookkeeping? Give us a call. International inheritance or insurance problems? Drop us a line. That winter we even managed to get somebody his damn inheritance out of Switzerland, where it was in probate. If you don't think *that* one's a miracle I won't even try you on my walking-on-water trick. In the same time we solved six cases of big-stakes arson, four murders, and a couple of extortion cases, one of them with international diplomatic implications.

Our biggest problem was administration. I ended up doing too much of it, with too little time in the field.

Then, at the beginning of the year, Burt Hooper, the former N17, took a spill out of a window, skiptracing a $500,000 embezzlement case in Buenos Aires. Burt was a real pro. He managed to make it around the corner and down the block to his car and drive all the way to the hospital before he collapsed. He'd busted one leg in six places, and they sent him back to New York in traction. It was okay. We'd been Mutt-and-Jeffing the office under consideration, and while the security people were going down that rickety fire escape looking for where the hell Burt could have got to, Burt's partner—a semiretired *Porteño* operative he'd hired on a one-shot basis—had got over the transom and got the goods on our man. Good old Burt. He never came back empty-handed.

I went by his hospital room, back in the States, and congratulated him. The leg, strung up in the air like that, looked like a very small dirigible getting ready to be launched. There was everything hanging from that damn ceiling but a flying trapeze.

He was taking it all badly. "Where's my goddam flowers?" he said.

"Here they are," I grunted. I heaved him a quart of 30-year-old scotch. He juggled it, but he caught it. "I would have got you a magnum or a jeroboam, but I wasn't sure where the hell you were going to hide it."

"Hide it hell. The nurse in charge has a hollow leg. She'll be matching me drink for drink before the shift's an hour old. She'll be glad to see this. The best I've been able to smuggle in before this was Chivas Regal."

"And here I was feeling sympathetic for you. Okay. If you're well enough to have the night nurse wrapped around your finger you're well enough to work for a living."

"Huh?" he said. He did a double-take. Then he caught my eye. "Hey. No way. No, god damn it, Carter, you try that one on me and—"

"What else can you do? Your second-story days are over for quite a few months now. What are you going to do with your time? Sit around and thumb through old copies of *Field and Stream?* Watch TV? Make model airplanes?"

"Look, I'm working on a method of jumping a nurse while in traction. When I'm done I'll take out the patent. I'll retire to Bimini on the proceeds and. . . ."

"Sorry. I got your release as of next Tuesday. It cost me, but the hospital administrator is on my side all the way. *He's* thinking of retiring to Bimini on what I slipped him."

"This is goddam slavery. Don't I get any choice in the matter? I'll quit. We don't have any contract anyhow. You can't hold me. I'll be out that damn door so fast. . . ."

I ignored him. "Look. I hired you an assistant."

"—No use trying to convince me. I—"

"She types 803 words a minute and she can take dictation even faster, and if she had three hands she could do both at the same time. She's the eighth wonder of the world. She—"

"I don't want to hear about it."

"She has total recall. She can remember the watermark on a piece of paper somebody filed with a shovel three years ago and four jobs back. She has an IQ off the top of the scale. They haven't tested anybody with an IQ high enough to test her."

"Yeah, and she looks like Marjorie Main after a nice rassle in the mud, I'll bet. You. . . ."

"She's a fifth dan black belt in Karate *and* judo, and placed third in an international pistol competition. She can do the 100 within a tenth of a second of the Olympic record, and she'd be at least a bronze medal in the decathlon if they'd let women compete."

"Bullshit. I know you, Carter. You're doing a number on me. Now she looks like Arnold Schwarzenegger and has a face like Elsie the cow. And if. . . ."

"Hey, Mame," I said. "You can come in now."

He looked over at the door. It opened. She came in. Mame Ferguson. She was everything I'd said and then some. She'd published three novels before she was 18, she played terrific jazz flute, and she'd walked out on the Miss Universe competition sometime back, when, as she said, "I suddenly thought, what am I doing here, strutting it for these assholes when I could be out having fun?" The other contestants had chipped in and sent her a box of candy in grateful appreciation.

What more can I say? She had coal-black hair and the smoothest tan you've ever seen, and big green eyes, and she was appealingly mammalian, and she had long legs—

"Hi, Burt," she said. Oh, I forgot. The voice was a dead ringer for what Peggy Lee sounded like when she was 25. Mame? She *looked* 25 . . . but how could she have done all those damn things—and yes, they were all for real, just as all of Mame that you could see was for real—and still be 25? Or 55 either, for that matter? Or 75?

I'd decided not to ask. "Nick. She's going to work for me?" Burt raised one brow. *"Her?"*

"How about it?" she said pleasantly—if that's the word. Even a mild question like that set off fireworks. "Am I? Or is he working for me?" She looked him up and down. Burt was a damned big handsome devil and the ladies usually didn't complain. This one wasn't complaining either.

"Oh, balls," I said. "You're both working for the sweat shop. If there's any pecking order you'll have to match nickels for it."

"Okay," she said with That Smile. "You run along now, boss. We'll work it out somehow. Is that a quart of scotch I see there? And nobody's thought of buying a lady a drink? Jesus Christ." She took the bottle from Burt's unprotesting hand, cracked the seal, and upended it for a snort. "Mmm," she said. "Here, Burt, have a pull at it.

Then I'll figure out some way we can arm wrestle for one-ups. Maybe if we reduced the angle of that rope up there on the right by ten degrees or so, and. . . ."

I waved goodbye. Burt gave me one last despairing glance. Then his eyes went back to Those Legs.

I went out the door feeling good—so good I walked all the way back to the office. Free! Free after 10,000 years in a bottle!

When I got back I found an urgent message on the Ansafone. I called Washington. An aide answered. I asked for Senator Mike Lovett. He was on in two shakes, sounding excited.

"Nick!" he said. "Am I glad to get hold of you!"

"You sound like a man with a problem, Senator. Shoot."

"Right. What's the first plane out for D.C.?"

"I dunno. From your tone it sounds like I oughta be on it."

"Yeah. Or whatever. A goddam Saturn rocket would be better. Whatever's fastest. Not a moment to lose. Big stuff. Big, *big* stuff."

"It always is, Mike. What is it?"

"Red alert," he said. That meant, among other things, that you couldn't talk about it on the phone.

"Huh. I'm persona non grata in Washington right now. And I don't do that kind of stuff any more. I'm a civilian now, remember?"

"Sure you do. Hell, don't let me down, Nick. There isn't anybody else that could handle it."

"Government stuff?" I sounded skeptical, I suppose.

"Yes—but not our government. Don't worry. If

anyone hassles you use that one phone call they give you to call me. Anybody that stands in the way I'll have his heart in aspic."

"Tight deadline, huh? When do you need it done, whatever it is?"

"Yesterday. God damn it, noon yesterday. Get on the plane, Nick. Call from La Guardia and I'll have a limo waiting at Dulles and you won't be able to tell the driver from Mario Andretti. And Nick."

"Yeah?"

"You'll need a woman operative. Somebody that looks like your kid sister—but tough as Wonder Woman."

"Okay." I hung up just as Mame was coming in the door. Kid sister? No way. There ought to be a word coined specially to describe what That Body did when it went through the door. "Walking" just didn't seem to describe it adequately.

"Hi, Nick," she said. "I think I'm going to like this job. How many operatives did you say you had?" She had a randy grin on her face, and That Voice was a purr.

"Check the file. Besides, three of them are women. And I need one of them now—call—damn it, all three of 'em are on duty. Mame, I need an op. Somebody demure and tough. No, don't give me That Look. You'd stick out in this gig like a neon sign in a nunnery. Do you know anyone? Tough type that can take care of herself?"

"I might," she said. "Tough, huh?"

"Yes, but kid sister. Naive. Central Casting naive."

"When do you need her?"

"In time to take off with me on the first plane to D.C."

"Give me half an hour on the phone. She'll meet you at the airport."

"That's my girl."

SEVEN

The phone rang as I was heading out the door. I stopped to watch her settle herself behind the big desk and answer it. It was Phone No. 2—*K. Masters Ltd., Industrial Troubleshooters.* As she picked up the phone I started again for the door—and something made me stop again.

"K. Masters," she said in a pleasant business voice as far from That Voice as you could possibly get. "Beg pardon? You. . . ."

Her red-nailed hand went over the receiver. "Nick. Get the extension. *Quick!*"

I dived for it and picked it up. " . . . Hello? Hello, Nick? Nick, is that you?"

The voice was Aggie Frye's. She'd been one of the best agents David Hawk—or I—had ever hired. The voice was taut and strained. "Yeah, Ag. Shoot it to me."

"Nick, I've got trouble. We've got trouble, all of us. Look, I've got only a moment, I think. I'm. . . ."

"Where are you?"

"Cleveland. Nick . . . I think I've bought the farm this time. They'll be busting in in a minute. I've got two shots left. I still don't know how I blew my cover. Unless . . . but no. Who'd be selling us out now? With AXE gone?"

"Ag. Calm down long enough to tell me. Who is it?" My mind raced. She'd been on what I was dead sure was an innocuous assignment, or as close to one as the business ever got. Straight industrial sabotage.

"Nick. It's old business from way back. Somebody's got a leftover hard-on for all of David's people. I was tailed. I took a slug in one arm. I'm getting weak. Arterial bleeding. I'd lost a lot of blood before I came out of it." Her voice was not her usual one: Aggie was sweet as sugar, usually, and tough as shoeleather. Now she sounded like a sick kid.

God damn it, *Cleveland*. I looked down at my balled fist, feeling impotent. "Aggie, honey, who is it?" God knows it could have been any one of a hundred groups that we'd crossed swords with. A lot of people—a *lot* of people—owed us a bad turn or two by now.

"Nick." The voice was fading. "Remember Code Name Pivot? Back in '63? I. . . ." That was all she got to say, though. There was a lot of background noise. A couple of loud bangs. The phone got itself dropped to the floor with a clatter.

I held the phone. I looked at Mame. Her eyes were wide. Not gee-whiz wide, just wide. So, I suppose, were mine. She was all attention, all concentration. I let out a deep breath. "See if the call can be traced."

"Right." She got on the wire. But it was too late. I sat looking at her, biting my lip. When she hung up in disgust she looked over at me. Her eyes were alert and concerned. "Nick. Is she. . . ?"

"I wouldn't be surprised," I said in a tight voice. "It's been known to happen. Look, sugar, can you get me. . . ." I stopped, thinking of the work sheet. "Hmm. Bill Stover's free, and he's in Chicago. Get him on this pronto. Damn. Damn. *Damn.*"

"Stover. Will do. What else?"

"That's enough. Read him the whole conversation as close to verbatim as possible. . . ."

"I can do it word for word, Nick. 98% total recall."

"Good girl. Let him handle it. He'll know what to do. And Mame."

"Yes?"

"See how many of the rest of the crew you can alert about this. Be sure to ask them about Code Name Pivot."

"What is it, Nick?"

"That's just it. I've never heard the phrase before in my life. Often nobody but Hawk and the agent in charge would have access to the information on a really tight covert operation. I'm gambling that at least one other agent was in on it."

"Okay. I'll ask everybody. Nick, this Mr. Hawk? What happened to him?"

"I don't know. I sure wish I did. I intend to ask in Washington. Although if David wanted to retire, he could move in right next door to you and disappear into the wallpaper." There wasn't much more to say about Hawk. Except that whoever these Pivot people were, if they really wanted to pay off an old debt to AXE and its people, what better place to start than at the top?

And there we were, I told myself in the cab. Unless one of the boys in the field could land me some info about this Pivot thing I was pretty much stymied for now. One thing I was damn sure of, and that was that David Hawk wouldn't even have left a footprint anywhere in D.C., much less any files on anything. He'd have burned everything there was, and that wouldn't have been much. Hawk had had a pretty free hand with things as head of department, and most of the files there were had been kept right between the slightly juggy ears on that grizzled head of his. That'd always been enough for me, and a long string of Killmaster agents, and every American President since FDR.

Now? As for how good an idea that all was, well, I was of divided mind. I could sure use some reference right now. David Hawk, I was thinking, where the hell are you?

And I hoped against hope that those suspicions that had begun drifting through my mind were just that—suspicions.

At the airport I cleared two tickets through to D.C. And I sat down and read the paper, and had a hot dog and a glass of milk, and had my shoes shined, and. . . .

Damned if I saw anyone.

I looked at my watch. Thirty minutes to takeoff.

I got on the wire and called Mame.

"K. Masters."

"Hi, Mame. Nick. No show on your girl yet."

"Hold your horses. She'll be there when you need her."

"Okay. Don't let me down."

"I won't. Nick. I started calling. No soap so far. Nobody knows anything about—what we were talking about."

Good girl. No use bandying sensitive words about, any more than you had to. "Keep plugging. Did you get Stover?"

"Yes. He's on the way. I told him he had complete charge."

"You're doing fine so far."

"You ain't seen nothin' yet."

"Okay. Just make sure I get that chickie you promised me."

"She'll be there when you need her."

"Okay."

On the boarding dock there still wasn't anybody I'd have cast for the role—and nobody came sidling up to me dressed in any sexy Dietrich trenchcoat whispering provocative statements out of one side of her mouth either. Ninety percent of the flight was male. The rest? Two nuns, each sweet-faced and plain and sixty. A snotty eight-year-old kid and her portly nanny. A tall, frigid-looking blonde. I looked this last one over, her and her librarian hairdo, and hoped to God *this* wasn't what Mame had sent me.

Boarding time came and still nobody. I looked around with some annoyance, and finally showed my ticket to the guy in the uniform.

I saved her the window seat, whoever she was. I settled down into the comfortable 707 seat and waited for her to show. *She'll be there when you need her,* Mame had said.

I frowned. They were closing the doors. The red light was on, and so was the sign about smoking and seat belts.

I looked around. Still nobody. A stewardess materialized at my elbow, small and cute and looking like Karen Valentine. "Pardon me, sir—this other ticket—"

"Yeah," I said sourly. "I got stood up."

"Oh. Well, there's a lady in back who'd like to swap if it would be all—"

"Lady?" I said. "Where?" I stuck my head out into the aisle. The deadly-looking blonde, all ice and frost and sharp bones, was glaring at me.

Oh, my God, I thought. Mame, what have you done to me? "Jesus," I said. "Sure, send her up." The stewardess smiled and motioned to the blonde. She walked forward in those sensible shoes of hers. She scrambled past me into the window seat. Even her rear end was bony. I was expecting her to jangle when she sat down, but she managed it quietly enough.

"Thank you," she said. Her eyes caught mine for a moment. There was the faintest glint of something vaguely human in there. . . .

"Pardon me," I said. "You aren't—I mean, do you know a woman named—?" I looked at her. Jesus Christ, no. She froze over again instantly. She spent the rest of the flight looking out the window. Knees pressed closely together. Hands held primly in her lap.

When we landed in Washington—still nothing. We all walked through the long tunnel and the long hall and the big waiting room and stood out front where the cabs were . . . and nobody.

I was angry as hell. I was about to place a terminating call to Miss Ferguson when a small hand slipped under my elbow in a soft and unmistakeable caress.

I looked around, startled.

There was my little Karen Valentine stewardess, in demure mufti now, her bright eyes looking up at me. "Nick?" she said in a better-than-friendly tone. "Angela Negri. Mame sent me. I just went on six weeks' vacation with pay. Let's go."

I looked her up and down. She was little, but she looked all business. There was a lot of intelligence behind those big brown eyes, and a lot of determination too. "Okay, Angie," I said. "Let's go."

EIGHT

We were sitting in the cab and I was digging my sidearms—Wilhelmina, Hugo, Pierre—out of my bag and she was looking big-eyed at me. She wasn't gee-whiz either, and that was something I found oddly reassuring. I tucked Hugo and Pierre away and worked the slide on Wilhelmina; everything seemed to be in pretty good order, all in all.

"Here," I said. "You'll need some iron." I was just reaching for a little snubnose Beretta automatic when she put a hand on my arm.

"Hey," she said. "I brought my own." She opened her purse to give me a good but quick look at a little bulldog .32. "It isn't any more accurate at any range than the Beretta is," she said with an expert's air, "but it hits a little harder than those little bitty bullets do." She gave me that cutie-pie smile again. "Don't worry. I can hit anything you can with it."

"Trust Mame," I said. I looked up and saw the driver shooting quick glances at us in the rear-view mirror. He had a concerned look on his face. "She didn't tell me anything about you."

"She told me lots about you," Angie Negri said. "Lucky Mame. She gets all the great jobs. I wished I looked like that."

"You'll do," I said. "Believe me. Now tell me about yourself."

"Okay," she said. "I went to college in Oregon and it bored the daylights out of me. I joined the Army and wound up with some time in the Language School at Monterey as an expert in Russian. It didn't do me a darn bit of good. I wound up working a non-language job with the NSA in Europe."

"Doing what?"

"There was a nice name for it, but the real gig was kidnapping people across the East German and Czech borders. I even got to do it once myself. I'm quick at languages. I picked up both tongues, accent-free, in no time. Mostly I handled the logistics of the matter, not the muscle. Once I did the muscle part. It wasn't any harder than the other part. A lot less dangerous too."

"Okay. You run into Mame in the business?"

"Yes. She was senior to me." I reminded myself to find out something about Angie's age; it would answer me some questions about Mame's. "Then, well, there were cutbacks. We got sent back to the States. I took out a private investigator's license in Washington, but I still had an itchy foot. I love to travel. I went to work for the airline in security. Hijack protection. The cover is that cute stewardess uniform. I fly wherever the airline flies. I've got friends around the world now. I may even learn to live with jet lag."

"Sounds great."

"I'm bored to death. When Mame brought up the job I jumped at it. You wouldn't want a permanent operative, would you?"

"Maybe," I said, sitting back and looking into those cute brown eyes. "Let's see how we do, both of us, on this job."

"Fair enough. Mame didn't tell me anything about it." Her eyes went to the window; then her head swiveled around toward the rear window. Her voice didn't change at all. "You had noticed: we're being tailed."

I hadn't. "Good catch," I said. I turned casually to her and looked around out of the corner of one eye. There was a big Lincoln Continental behind us, keeping pace, no more. "Wouldn't be surprised if you're right," I said. "Did Mame mention the . . . ah . . . recent trouble?"

"Sort of. Somebody killed up in Ohio somewhere."

"Right. Old enemies. Whether this is the same folks . . . well. . . ." I smiled at her and spoke louder, to the driver. "Hey, pal, can you shake that car behind us?"

"Shake him?" he said. "You mean. . . ?"

"What will this thing do?"

"Oh. That." He hit the accelerator. There was some soup under the hood of that dumpy old Chevy. The car shot forward. "Huh," he said. "Look at that. They're stickin' with us."

I looked around, casual no more. "Okay. Floor it. I'll pay the bills if you get busted. Just get us the hell out of here."

The big car behind us gained ground. No matter how much junk our cab had under the hood, the

Continental could match it.

"Nick," she said. "You think it's the—?"

"I don't know," I said. As I looked back the big car blinked its lights: the pattern—on-off-on, pause on-off-on, pause, on-off-on, long pause.

"Hey," I said to the driver. "Slow down. It's friends. Slow down. Pull over onto the shoulder. Stop."

"But Nick. . . ."

"It's okay," I told her. And it was. When we stopped the big black car pulled up behind us. Two guys in those damn hungup-looking FBI suits came up and opened our door.

"Mr. Carter?"

"Yes."

"Senator Lovett's compliments. If you'd just join us in the staff car. . . ." I grinned. I'd almost forgotten Mike's driver—the one you wouldn't be able to tell from Mario Andretti.

"Come on, Angie," I said, handing the cabbie a medium-sized greenback. "It's okay. We're among friends."

Barker and Lipton were all business. They hardly even noticed Angie. That's the FBI for you. "We wanted to bring you in, Mr. Carter, because of—well, the situation in D.C. regarding people from your old branch. . . ."

"I understand," I said. "Maybe you guys can do me a favor sometime. Matter of fact—"

"Glad to," Barker said. He was the talkative one. Lipton hadn't opened his kisser so far. "God knows we've used your outfit in the past when we couldn't get the word on something otherwise. We probably owe you a few favors."

"Okay. I can't get at some records—if they exist

anymore. If they haven't been destroyed, the Bureau ought to be able to wangle access."

"Shoot," Barker said. He was about as bland a guy as you'd ever meet—a perfect FBI agent. You'd forget the face five minutes after you saw it.

"Code Name Pivot," I said. "I need the file on the activity. It seems somebody on the bad guy side just knocked off a good operative of mine, and she gave me the codeword before they got to her. The only other person that's likely to know—among my circle, anyhow—is gone."

"That'd be Hawk, whatever it is," Barker said. "Good man. Good cop. Very good cop."

It was stretching a point, but yeah—David would have liked to hear the Bureau calling him a good cop. "I'm curious," I said. "If the Bureau files had anything on his present whereabouts. . . ."

"I'll see what I can learn," Barker said. "You'll be in town—how long?"

"As little as possible," I said. "Mike Lovett said this was triple-rush stuff. He'll likely have me out of the office and on the road as soon as I've had time to be briefed. But if you could maybe phone it in to my number"—I gave him the "K. Masters" card—"on your Watts line as soon as you've got it, the folks there can get me the word fairly fast."

"Sure," the FBI man said. "Glad to be of help."

So far, Lipton beside him on the seat hadn't said a damn thing.

They didn't bother taking us up to the Hill. The Continental instead went up Connecticut Avenue and pulled into the taxi stand at the Shoreham Hotel. From there we were sent up the freight elevator to the fourth floor and down a back hall. Lipton walked ahead of us, Barker behind. Both of them wore their right hands up high where they could pluck at a button idly as they walked—or grab for a pistol if they had to.

We stopped at a door. Lipton knocked, a curious passwordy kind of knock. We were shown in.

The place was a suite of rooms used from time to time by certain influential people in the Senate for confidential discussions. The last one I'd heard of had been used by somebody rigging a plea-bargain for one of the Koreagate guys if he'd testify before the investigating committee.

Mike Lovett came out of the back room. Angie's Karen Valentine smile was big-eyed and looked properly impressed. I rushed introductions all around. Mike, his famous company manners much in evidence, gave Angie an appreciative look and raised one eyebrow at me appreciatively.

"Don't worry about her," I said. "Way I understand it, she can take care of herself. You gave me the typecasting, remember?"

Lovett waved a well-manicured hand. His manner was flawless. One of these damn years he'd be making a serious bid for the Presidential nomination. With those Mr. Integrity looks he might just make it. "All right. Just . . . well, watch out for her. She'll need all the help she can get." He sat down on the couch across from us, reached for a file in his briefcase and handed it over.

I spread it out between us.

Shiekh Achmed.

He was one of the most important people in the world. He was the one man who could hold the balance of power in the Mideast conflict in his hand. He was advisor to the King of Arabia and virtually all of the smaller oil shiekhdoms in the Crescent on matters of oil pricing. He had single-handedly kept the world price of oil down during the last two OPEC meetings by virtue of his powerful influence on virtually every Muslim leader in the Middle East.

He could start a global war overnight—or grind it to a halt by cutting off the combatant's supply of petroleum.

I whistled long and low. Angle, looking up, caught my eye and made a small silent *wow* with those pretty lips. "So?" I said.

"So what about him?" Lovett said. We stayed sitting; he rose and paced back and forth as he spoke. "Look, if this weren't important—you can see how important—you know I wouldn't have brought you back. You know what the situation is about having you guys back in town. If somebody caught me bringing you in right now they'd crucify me. Senate and all. Hell, I couldn't land in worse trouble if they caught me molesting a kid in the middle of the F Street Mall at midday, with the TV cameras grinding away. Nick—"

"I'm waiting for you to drop that other shoe," I said.

"Damn. Okay. Look. I didn't ask you here. There's no damn government connection at all. Understand? Jake Quitman's footing the bill. As a patriotic gesture. He—"

"Jake?" I said, sitting up. "What's Jake got to do with this?"

Lovett was getting agitated. "Damn it, Nick. Look. You got Jake's girl out of Mexico. Out of one of those international white-slave rings. He's grateful. He's patriotic. He's a big party contributor. He . ."

"I'm waiting."

"Nick. This Sheikh Achmed. He's due in town in one week from today. His schedule is tight as a drum. He'll only have twenty-four hours in Washington. He'll be flying in from the oil conference and will fly back immediately to the Geneva peace talks. We're at a delicate point right now. We've got the Israeli and Egyptian leaders ready to sit down at the bargaining table again for the first time in . . . hell, I don't know how long. And the Syrians are raising hell, and that crazy bastard Khoumeni is starting to meddle, and the one thing in the world that can keep the present situation from erupting into a full-scale—possibly global—conflict is the presence of Sheikh Achmed, rested and fit and in a good mood, at the peace talks. . . ."

"So?"

"So. . . ." He wiped his brow. His face grew more and more agitated. His voice grew more constricted. "Sheikh Achmed has a daughter, the apple of his eye. He dotes on the girl. She's been in private school here."

"Yeah?"

Lovett stopped pacing and looked at us, one after the other. "Nick. She's disappeared. Disappeared from the face of the earth."

I leaned forward, beginning to get the picture. "And you think—"

"She's been snagged by the slavers. Same damn kind of people that grabbed the Quitman girl. Only we don't have any idea from what country, or where they've taken her. She's just plain damn disappeared."

I whistled long and low. "And what happens when the Sheikh comes to town and expects to see his happy, virginal little daughter waiting for him at the airport?"

He didn't answer me. He rolled his eyes heavenward. But there was no comedy in the gesture. No comedy at all. "Big Casino," he said. "Checkmate." His eyes were downright desperate. "Bingo."

NINE

Somebody called Mike to the phone. I looked over at Barker and Lipton; they were huddled in the corner. I caught Angie's big brown eye. "Hey," I whispered. "Keep an eye on me. Do what I do. Stay alert."

"Why?" she said. But she was looking very heads-up when she said it.

"Somebody doesn't want us to stick around D.C. too long—not even those two or three hours' worth that I'd already budgeted us for."

"Well?"

"Well, I'm a taxpayer too. By year's end I'll be a damn Three-Eye League version of a major taxpayer. Nobody tells me I gotta stay out of the Capital of the United States."

"I dig. What are you going to do?"

"Give Uttmay and Effjay over there the Ipslay."

"I'm with you." I was getting to like her smile. And my opinion of Mame had gone up some, even since that morning. I looked Angie over now. She couldn't be over five-one or so without those high heels, and she'd come in at about 90 pounds. I thoroughly approved of the way somebody'd allocated the pounds: slim here, broad there, everything nice and firm.

As Mike came back into the room, I asked him whether the girl left any kind of trail behind.

"Yeah," Mike said. He reached in a pocket and handed me an envelope. "She did. There are two girls involved. She and her roommate—a girl named Sandy Fleischer. Sandy was stage-struck. We think she took off for New York to audition for this thing. We think she talked our missing girl into going with her. Neither of them has been seen since."

I opened the envelope. There were photos marked Sandy Fleischer (thin, redheaded, intense-looking: a young Julie Harris type) and Meriem Mouchamel. The last . . .

Well, they like 'em lush in the Arab countries, even the young ones. This one was a young Sophia Loren, only with those dark flashing eyes, almost black, that you never find outside of the Middle East—except sometimes in gypsy girls. A real beauty, striking, unforgettable. Not rock-and-roll skinny, either. *Saftig*—or whatever they call it on the Arab side of the border.

I passed it over to Angie, who read the clip that accompanied the pix. It was pretty standard in the sex-slavery business. *Dancers wanted, will train, for troupe touring France, Italy, Mediterranean ports. Passport needed.*

I sighed and handed that one over too. I'd already done a batch of research both before and after the Quitman case. All it took to get my dander up was to think about what I'd read for a bit.

"You're right, Senator," Angie said. "This is a job for a woman. It's the only way. You won't be able to get in. Only me. The ad is still current. There're three days left to register."

She stood up, looking cute as a button. That was the damned tough part about it. She *did* look like your kid sister—or a sexy version of her. You wanted to protect her. "She's been gone . . . how long?"

"Three days," Lovett said.

"And you're pretty sure this is what's happened?"

"We've got testimony from people who gave the two a ride to New York. Sandy was talking about it the whole way." He glared at us. "This is a free country. You can take out any kind of ad you want to, in any kind of paper you want to. This one was clipped from a respectable trade journal. We found it in the hotel room they rented when they got to New York."

"Do we know anything about this outfit that took out the ad?" I asked.

"Not much," Barker said, moving forward now. "We have a mailing address in Monaco. It seems to be some sort of primary dispersion point." He handed over a piece of paper with an address on it: *Hotel Splendide, Monte Carlo.* I handed it to Angie; she took it in and handed it back to Barker. I knew she'd memorized it already. "I'm sure your man Hawk would have had a file on it, but. . . ."

"God damn it," I said. "God damn it to hell. Okay. Okay, Angie." I gave her a look, then shot my eyes at the window. Neither of the agents saw it, and I was pretty sure Mike had missed it too.

"Look, I've got to go to the john. I'll see you in a moment. Meanwhile, you ask Mike what there is to be known about these two kids. Okay?" I made sure nobody was looking and then I gave her a big wink. She nodded perhaps a millimeter.

I went inside the big bathroom of the suite. It was a matter of moments to get the jammed window open and slip out of it. I closed it again behind me and climbed down the stone wall of the hotel to the ground. Angie exited in a more conventional manner and joined me about a minute later.

"Nick," she said. "There was a dossier on the two girls in the file. When they weren't looking I copped it." She patted her bag. "We can look at it in the cab." One of which was idling nearby—and quickly acquired two passengers.

I gave Downtown a wide berth. I sent the driver way the hell over to Georgetown and had him drop us a few blocks from a car rental agency—just far enough away so that he wouldn't make the connection if asked.

We rented a car and drove up the Interstate toward Baltimore, figuring we'd make New York by evening. Going through Baltimore, however, we wound up making a stop at Haussner's Restaurant, with the world's largest menu, some of the best seafood anywhere, and the world's worst collection of original art. We got to know each other a little better, looking across a table full of wonderful food at each other.

I paused just before the cheesecake and went out to make a call.

"T. Woodman," the voice said. That Voice.

"You're staying late," I said. "I didn't expect to find you in, Mame."

"Nicky! Did Angie find you?"

"Yeah. We're heading north. Did you hear anything from—"

"Agent Barker of the Bureau called. He congratulates you on getting away."

"Did he give you anything about Code Word Pivot?"

"Yes. A little. The records are all destroyed. But he did find someone in the records department who vaguely remembers the file, somebody who had to pull it for Hawk once. Apparently Pivot was the code word for some kind of terrorist activity. There was a tie-in with Black September, and the Japanese group, and Baader-Meinhof."

"That's all? No more?"

"It stopped right about there. I've alerted everybody. Nick. You watch out too. You and Angie."

"I think she'll do all right. I may wind up offering her a job. If she's as tough a customer as you say she is . . . well, she's cool enough, I can say that already."

"She'll be there when you need her."

"Okay," I said. *"Ciao."* I hung up.

A small pair of arms came up behind me. It was Angie, and the way she pressed that pint-sized—but surprisingly voluptuous—little body against me I suddenly had other ideas than cheesecake. I turned and held her. She held up a doggy bag in one hand. "Don't worry," she said in a voice full of mischief, "I *got* the damn cheesecake. For afterward. . . ."

I bent and kissed her. And let me tell you, size doesn't mean a damn thing. Inside that tiny body there was a big, lusty, voluptuous broad just begging to be let out. I gave her a squeeze and reminded myself to let her out, and soon.

She read my mind again. "Come on," she said. "I just used that other phone over there to make a room reservation at a place up north of Towson."

Angie.

She came out of the bathroom with a couple of towels draped over her. She was so tiny that two of the things made a sarong for her. I handed her a glass of something wet. "Here," I said. *"Zdorowie pana."*

Her smile was warm and appealing. Her eyes had bedroom shining right out of them. *"Prost,"* she said. She tipped the glass. "You yank on that little knot up there, first, like—like *that* . . . Mmmmm. *Mmmmm.* . . . Then you untwist this one down there . . . yes . . . yessss. . . ."

Angie. . . .

The light was soft and dim and sexy. In it that tiny body was bronzed and lovely, like a beautiful statuette. The body wasn't petite at all. She *was* a big broad, full-breasted and voluptuous. She was just scaled down. With a groan she put the glass down and stepped into my arms. Her grip on my back was strong and assertive.

I picked her up and carried her over to the big bed. She was light as a feather, soft as goosedown, hard as spring steel. And tireless, hungry, abandoned.

* * *

I woke up, blinking.

Something was wrong.

Angie was gone.

I got up and ran to the dressing table. There was a note on it:

> Sorry, Nick. This is a woman's job. I need a day's lead on you and this is the only way to get it. Come and get me and we'll pick up where we left off. I'll find the kids; you find me.
>
> Love, Angie

TEN

That, however, was the cue to take the hell off for New York in a hurry. I had no idea how she'd gone up, or when, and the main thing was to get on her tail in a hurry.

I called Mame.

"K. Masters, good morning."

"Hi, baby. Nick. Angie gave me the slip. She's gone in to answer that goddam want ad herself. The one that—"

"Yeah, I know. I pumped Barker."

"Okay. Did he give you the address and phone number?"

"No. Shoot." I passed it over. "I'll get right on it."

"No. Make an appointment, but I don't want you out of the office right now. You get me? Somebody has to coordinate calls from the field. Burt Hooper won't be out of the hospital for another week."

"The hell he won't. I had a little talk with the

administrator. Where are you?"

"North of Baltimore, heading north. What do you mean, had a talk with the administrator?"

"By the time you're here Burt will be on duty. They're moving him in here, in traction, cute nurse and all. I, ah, exerted some influence," she said in That Voice again. I could almost see her randy grin. "Look, Nick, you didn't think I was going to miss all this fun and games, did you?"

"Damn it, who's running this outfit?"

"The IRS, of course, just like any other business. Nick: I'll call the number and set up an appointment, giving you plenty of time to get here. How about three p.m.?"

"Fine. I'll call you when I get in."

"I've been checking the traffic reports. Go over to Staten Island at Elizabeth and come across through Brooklyn over the Narrows Bridge. You're maybe two hours out. There's a big wreck near the tunnel entrance and you'd better go around."

"That's my efficient girl. I'll burn up some tires." I hung up and then gave the desk a call, asking for the bill and for someone to bring the car around. I was shaving when the explosion went off. It shook the whole motel. I ran around to the front window and stood looking down at the mess in the parking lot—but somehow I didn't have to ask whose car it was. I'd known the moment the explosion had sounded. I looked down at the blackened, immobile arm sticking out of the mass of bright flames and black smoke that had been my rented Pinto and winced. I'd sent some poor devil to his death, asking for a pickup on the car. Innocent people, now. Well, I'd been mad before, but it was nothing to the mad I was getting on. Code Name Pivot, look out. . . .

When I called her again it was from a pay phone on Staten Island. She gave me an address in the mid-Sixties, and a half-hour's lead. I got back in the little Toyota I'd rented in Towson and dogged it all the way into town.

She met me downstairs. She wasn't the same Mame. I don't know what I was expecting, but I certainly wasn't prepared for her looking demure. "Don't have a heart attack on me," she said. "It's just your little old office girl."

The modern equivalent of pinafore and bobby sox, New York style, was a leotard and a pair of jeans and the kind of sandals that lace up the side of your leg. She looked like somebody coming in from modern dance class at the YWHA. That beautiful hair was in a long, long braid. "So help me God," I said. "If you hadn't winked I'd have walked right on by. Even at that I thought you were just giving me a come-on."

"All in the day's work. Now let's go flummox these sons of bitches.

We took the same elevator up, but I stopped one floor below her and walked the rest of the way. She was inside the office by the time I came up, and there was nothing to do but wait out in the hall for her signal.

Or was there, now? I tried the door—softly, gently—but it was locked. Then I had a look at the next office. The sign on the door said *M. Ophee, Imported Music,* but by the time I'd picked the lock and let myself inside it was obvious Mr. Ophee hadn't been around in a couple of weeks. I went across the room, opened his window, and crawled out on the ledge. I was fourteen floors up, but I didn't look down. Across the street a secretary looked out her window and saw me. Her eyebrows went up; then she went back to her filing. Nothing short of a major earthquake could have disturbed her bored expression.

When I drew up to the next window I could see the back of the guy's head as he sat before the window, talking to her. She was alert as hell, as usual; she spotted me before I'd had time to blink, and went to work. She stood up and moved back a few steps onto the bare floor and began doing an improvised dance routine, right out of a 1943 Judy Garland movie. Gee, Mr. Schmutzblum, do you really think I could be a star?

I slipped the window up—but he felt the draft and turned. He reached inside the desk for a big nickelplated gun. I could see it right there.

I swung the window open all the way. I still wasn't going to be fast enough to stop him. The gun fairly leaped into his hand.

And leaped back out again. Mame had clobbered his right forearm with some sort of dumbass statuette she'd picked off his desk. God almighty, could she move fast—and I swear she did it all without skipping a beat in that crazy dance improvisation of hers. She slugged him on the neck with the thing, again right on the downbeat, and that gave me time to scramble inside.

He went to his knees with that one, but recovered and came at me. He walked right into a stiff right. It sat him back down again. I picked him off the floor by his tie and shoved him into the corner, kicking him once in the pills just to show him I had jacks or better.

"Gee," she said. "You men and your damned stupid supermacho bullshit. You guys keep hitting people with your fists, and you know how easy it is to break a finger that way."

"What's he said so far?"

"He—Oh, my God." She looked at her perfectly-in-character $11.95 *Star Wars* watch and sighed. "The last batch took off on a plane half an hour ago. From Kennedy. For Marseilles."

"Damn," I said, meaning it. I grabbed him by the lapels and hauled him to his feet. He was still looking a little grey under that five o'clock shadow, but I didn't have time to wait. "Okay, you. Where are they bound for? Give me some addresses right away, and some names, or—"

"I—Hotel Splendide, Monte Carlo. Room 400. You—"

"Okay, damn it. Let's hear some more. That's the dispersion point. Where do they go from there?"

"I don't know," he said. I busted his nose with a looping overhand right. "Oh. Oh, my God. I—" I feinted another. "No, please!" He held his hand to his face and talked, painfully. "This is—you're right. The dispersion point has been Nice for many years now. Recently . . . recently the *Sûreté* has begun a campaign. Already our Marseilles operation has been temporarily closed down. . . ."

"Temporarily? That means you're still operating. From where? Give me some names quick, and some addresses, or—"

"No. Please." He reeled off some names, and a

street number on *La Cannebiere*, the ancient ropemakers' street of the old seaport. I shot Mame a glance. She was taking it all down on a notebook she'd produced from that enormous handbag she'd brought alone.

"Now let's get back to the shipments. These last girls . . . where are they headed? And what about the two chicks that came in . . . uh . . . four days ago?" I shot him a quick description of Sandy Fleischer and Meriem Mouchamel, and feinted another wallop at his nose when he slowed down a bit.

In the end we didn't get a lot from him. He'd been just the contact man—the guy who signed 'em up. They'd kept him pretty much in the dark about the other end of the operation. He was working at a piecework rate, two hundred dollars a girl. When he came out with that rate Mame was ready to sock him one on the snout herself.

I pulled him together—he was limp and manageable by now—and pushed him ahead of me. "Mame. He's got to be delivered to the cops. We've got to stop it at this end. But I need a day's lead. Otherwise we'll blow things here and let them know I'm coming on the other end. That way it's likely to be curtains for Angie and the kids."

"Okay," she said. "I know someplace we can stash him for a day before delivering him. You've got your lead." She stopped to retrieve his gun and his appointment book before following the two of us to the door. It was virtually all there was in the big desk, and the room was otherwise bare—not even a file cabinet.

I opened the door and shoved him ahead of me into the hall.

There was a scuffling noise in the hall.

The man in front of me burst into flames!

He got off a couple of quick groans, and staggered forward into the wall. I could hear feet running down the hall. I stuck my head out—and saw a pair of legs hightailing it around the corner. "Mame!" I said. "Grab him. Put the fire out." Before I'd finished the sentence I was sprinting after the firebug—but by the time I reached the corner he was gone.

I looked back. Whatever they'd thrown on him was deadly stuff. Mame couldn't even get close to him. The heat was enormous. It was like those terrible pix you used to see in the papers back in the Vietnam days—the Buddhist monks burning alive in the streets. Only he wasn't dying serenely.

It wasn't nice to watch.

There was the possibility of a fire in the building. I figured the rest of the occupants didn't have any arson coming to them, whatever I might feel about this poor bastard who was frying to death on the marble floor before us. I doused him with a cuspidor full of sand and let him smolder.

"Okay," I said. "Let's get the hell out of here before anybody comes through that elevator door."

Mame started to say something. She looked down at the guy on the floor, who was past all caring. She bit her lip once and then looked at me. There was a new hard glint in her eye. "You're right. He didn't deserve any better. Lead on, boss."

We slipped down the stairs to the fifth floor, then took the elevator. I walked her down the street a block, arm in arm, and then, when the crowd had thinned out a little, pulled her out of the stream of traffic into a storefront that sported a dusty-looking "Closed" sign.

"Okay," I said. "This is where we split up. Get back to the office and into your Mame outfit. Stay on top of things. You're in charge, baby. Burt thinks he's the big cheese while I'm gone and you don't want to hurt his feelings, but you and I will know better. You know as much as I do right now about Code Name Pivot. You know enough to look out for yourself." And given their apparent methods, I hoped I was placing my trust in the right person.

ELEVEN

Six days left. And by the time I touched down in Nice, five days.

There's only one thing sure about this kind of work, and that's the inescapable fact that you can't do the job if you're dead.

That's why, when I rented a Citroën in Nice, I gave the matter a bit of thought before taking that nice spectacular ocean highway, with its fabulous view—and its equally fabulous curves, microscopic shoulders, and sheer drops to the rocks above that gorgeous blue Mediterranean below.

That's why, when I had a look at the road map which showed me the four main routes that covered the twelve as-the-crow-flies kilometers to Monte Carlo, I decided to go inland, through the valley of the Laghet, and cut down through La Turbie. For one thing, Highway N204 has a lot less traffic. If anybody were to get the notion of following me, I wouldn't have a hell of a lot of doubt about the matter, the way I would if my pursuer tried to tail me in the middle of that gaudy procession of Lancias and Aston-Martins and Ferraris that plied N559 most any hour of the day or night.

And the funny thing was, I had a strong notion I *was* being tailed. All the way from the boarding dock on my L-1011 back at Kennedy, right to the moment the Boulevard de Risso ran into the Turin route and became N204.

Don't ask me how I knew, back on the plane. You can lose a tail damn easy on one of those wide-body horrors. They can also lose you, but it's harder.

Now? I drove slowly up the nice modern road that followed the slow curves of the Paillon, watching. And sure enough, before I'd gone five kilometers I'd picked up somebody in a black Mercedes. I speeded up. He speeded up. When I turned east, leaving the main road, he turned east with me.

All of those roads east are fairly precipitous, and full of curves. Trying to race on any of them is stupid as hell. That doesn't stop anybody in that part of the world. This is, after all, Grand Prix country, and people who'd throw high-speed road races through the cobbled streets of a town whose roads were obviously laid out by a cow are capable of anything but common sense.

So when I kicked the accelerator up, the guy behind me stayed with me. When I started taking curves on two wheels and a prayer, he did too. After a while it became evident he was gaining on me.

I did the only thing to do just then. I slowed down. I slowed to a respectable French-papa-on-a-Sunday-drive speed. I shot a glance at the rear-view mirror from time to time to see if anyone had a gun aimed at my head, and the two guys in the car didn't seem to.

I slowed a little more—and stationed myself smack dab in the middle of the road, straddling the white line. I slowed to twenty km/hr.—fifteen. . . .

Finally I came to a stop. I looked back in the mirror. Somebody was getting out of the righthand door.

I let him get all the way to the back bumper of the Citroën. Then I hit the accelerator and started speed-shifting. First—second—third—

I sneaked a look back at them. The outside man had had to scramble back to the car. This gave me just enough edge to gain some ground on them as the road started climbing. Soon I could see the cross atop Notre Dame de Laghet, and I hit the turn just outside of the tiny village in a racing skid.

Now it was all hill-climb stuff, as the road climbed steadily through the olive groves toward La Turbie and the spine of the coast range, making literally hundreds of hairpin turns. Mt. Bataille loomed on my left, Mont Camps-de-l'Alle on my right. The tires squealed.

On a switchback I could see him laboring with the curves in his much heavier car. The road hadn't been built for a Mercedes. Hell, it hadn't even been built for cars—or horses either. The Romans built it for four soldiers to march abreast on a through route from Genoa to Gaul. In 6 B.C., Augustus hadn't had to worry about anybody skidding on bald tires. As I barreled headlong through La Turbie, scattering pigs and chickens before me, I could look up and see the Doric colonnade old Octavian had had built to praise himself, sitting proudly at the top of the pass . . . and now I could see the

Mediterranean, and Monte Carlo, below me, and in the mirror behind I could see no sign at all of the Mercedes. I shrugged. I'd meet them again, I had no doubt—hopefully under better circumstances.

Monaco.

Preposterous. Ridiculous. Absurd. The silliest idea for a country I'd ever seen. Population about 35,000—but physically about the size of Chitlin Switch, Georgia. Eight square miles of expensive land surrounding a trapezoidal body of sheltered water you could shoot a .22 rifle across. Katharine Hepburn once referred to it as "a pimple on the chin of France."

Me? I've always been crazy about it. Maybe it's the underdog thing. Maybe it's the fact that it's got to be the only nation in the whole world that doesn't have any slums. You drive past those imposing facades expecting any minute to see them turn out to be movie-set houses, with no rear end, propped up with two-by-fours. They aren't. Everything's real. That's the crazy part. It goes back to the 13th century, and somehow it managed to miss all the serious manifestations of history—although France briefly annexed it during the Revolution, only to lose it in one of the Congress of Vienna hassles. 1870? 1914? 1939? All of them passed it by. The big historical figures here are not Hitler and De Gaulle. They're Mata Hari, who shot a Russian colonel on the Casino grounds when she caught him fiddling with her fried eggs; and King Farouk; and Onassis.

The language, of course, is French, although the ruling family is Italian and Irish-American. There's no tax and no draft.

It's also refreshingly free of certain business restraints, which attracts, let us say, certain elements. One of them is arms: the world's biggest dealer in the implements of war has his headquarters here—as did his predecessor. There are certain advantages to moving a certain kind of business here, the way there are certain advantages to incorporating your firm in Delaware or starting your family foundation in the District of Columbia. The shark mentalities hear about this sort of jazz damn fast. They head here like a shot out of a gun once the advantages have been explained to them.

Apparently the international trade in girls had heard of those advantages recently—and zeroed in on the little principality like so many other sharks had.

That kind of crowd wouldn't operate out of the Hotel de Paris, where Escoffier set up the kitchen and planned the menus. You wouldn't find them at the Metropole or the Hermitage either. Matter of fact, they wouldn't be working either the Rock of Monaco or the Casino area itself. They'd be down in the flat, where the shore highway from Nice divides La Condamine, the port area, from the new industrial suburb of Fontveille.

That was where the Hotel Splendide turned out to be. It wasn't grubby. Nothing in Monaco is grubby. What it was was new. And in Monaco, anywhere of the four tiny divisions that make it up, new is automatically one step down the social ladder—whether you're a business or an heiress. The dough has to be so old nobody in the business, or the family, can remember the ignominious things that had to be done in the course of making it.

I turned the little car in at the local offices of the

rental agency and took a taxi to the Splendide. In a way it was nice. It wasn't one of the biggies like the Hotel de Paris; they have much tougher security.

It was pushing noon when I registered—as Mr. Carter Nickerson, of Sioux Falls, owner of a prosperous import-export and mail-order business. I'd taken some pains to figure out how the numbers worked on the hotel, and I'd wound up with No. 500, immediately above the one in question.

I felt pretty good. I thought I'd go grab some lunch before getting down to work. I turned back toward the desk on the way out . . . and stopped.

There was somebody looking at the register while the clerk's back was turned. He had the book turned around. . . .

I'd seen him before. He'd just got finished chasing me half the hell the way here from Nice—and I'd got a good look at him when he'd got out of the car.

What the hell. I strolled out into the street and headed down toward La Condamine. Monaco can be appallingly expensive if you have it in your head that the only place to eat is someplace like the *Ambassadeurs* or Rampoldi's or the Grill Room. If what you want is just plain decent seafood, or stick-to-the-ribs country French cooking, a fine meal can still be had at a moderate price, even with the way the buck has been sinking on the world market.

I found something even better. Since the Vietnam conflict, one of the big surprises both in America and Europe has been the new growth of Southeast Asian restaurants. I hadn't gone five blocks when I ran across a brand-new, spotlessly clean Thai restaurant called the *Krung Tep.* I slipped inside and ordered ginger beef and a nice tofu dish.

And looked around me. . . .

The joint was all but deserted. There were two fortyish old maid types sitting in the corner, wearing the kind of clothes you can only get by with at twenty-five. There was a burly, thick-set man sitting with his back to me, wearing a beret the way they wear them over there—hanging down the back of his neck. I could watch the heavy muscles in his shoulders move as he manipulated his chopsticks.

I ordered a beer. No luck on those gorgeous Bangkok beers: around here you were lucky if you could get a half-assed Alsatian brew like Kronenbourg.

Two men came in at the door.

I recognized both of them this time. My friends from the car.

They looked around, very carefully avoiding looking at me.

The waiter came with the beer. "I'll be right back," I said. "I have to get something from the car." I took one sip of beer just for the hell of it and then went out the door.

I didn't head for the street. I headed around to the alley. I wanted somebody to follow me.

I'd just slipped into the alley and turned around to face whoever came after me when somebody clobbered me with something hard. I half-turned, my eyes dancing with bright colored lights, and slipped to one knee.

The guy from the black car had come through a

side door in the joint. His pal was right there beside him. I hit the ground and rolled away from him, hoping to buy a blink or so of time. The man with the sap stepped forward. His friend pulled a big Russian-made revolver from a shoulder holster under his coat.

I was reaching for Wilhelmina, still groggy, but my fingers felt like a string of sausages: no bones, no muscles. Inert.

And then damned if the guy from the restaurant —the heavy-set one with the beret—didn't step out into the alley, take a gander at what was going on, and go into action. There was a wagon full of fresh trays of French bread, ready for delivery, beside the door, and they were the kind that comes long as your arm and with a nice hard finish on the outside that keeps the stuff nice and moist inside. He selected one and, unhurriedly, swung it around like Reggie Smith taking a cut at a Tom Seaver fast ball.

It caught the gunman right on the septum. The gun went off—right by my ear—and fell from his hands. By that time I had Wilhelmina out—but the fellow who'd slugged me gave me a good *savate* kick in the wrist and my faithful old prewar Luger went flying into the dirt alongside that Spanish revolver. Then the man who'd taken the bread in the kisser—he was bleeding like a stuck pig—got up and the two of them ran for it, down the alley and around the corner.

The stocky man watched them go. I gave him a look. He looked tough, good-humored, dangerous. The type of guy who'd convince you that fifty-five was the prime of life. His nose had been broken a few times and pushed first this way, then that. I'd known a guy in the States who looked like that, an old L.A. boxfighter named Art Aragon. If his nose got in the way he could tuck it in either his left ear or his right. It didn't make a damn.

This guy looked like that—only intelligent.

"*Alors, monsieur,*" he said—and then, reconsidering, switched to English. "Come back and enjoy your lunch." He motioned at the door with one polite hand the size of an outfielder's glove: the gesture held a lot of humor and couldn't have been more eloquent if he'd said aloud *Aprês toi, mon cher Alphonse.*

I grinned at him, rubbing my neck where the guy had hit me. "*Au contraire,*" I said. "*Aprês toi, mon cher Gaston.*" I showed him the way. He grinned back and didn't argue.

TWELVE

I'll skip the French. The conversation proceeded in it. "Hey, waiter," the stocky guy said, handing over the bread stick. "Somebody left this on your doorstep." He grinned. "*Monsieur* will move his lunch to my table."

The waiter raised an eyebrow, but nodded. The heavyset man led me to a seat opposite his. "Not many people come here for lunch yet. Just us old *Legion Étrangerè* vets. I was at Dienbienphu. Last plane out. We all used to take our leaves in Thailand. Sentimental stuff."

I sat down. I didn't know what to make of him, but I kind of liked him. "Everybody who ever ate Thai food came back for more," I said. "I've been in and out of Southeast Asia a few times myself." I shot him a hard glance. "You're an odd duck. Anybody else would have been hollering for the cops." I looked at his hand, with the chopsticks in it. That alone would have told me he was an old Vietnam or China hand. Only Chinese and Vietnamese—and people who served there—ate Thai food with sticks as he and I did. It's a regional habit of a sort. Thais themselves eat with forks and spoons.

"Why should I bother the *flics?*" he said with a shrug. "Unless you care about catching those two guys with the guns."

"Il n'y a pas de quoi," I said. "They were tailing me. Perhaps next time they'll catch up with me. Next time they won't catch me napping like that." I raised my glass of beer in a salute. "Thanks."

"Pas de fuoi," he said, but he acknowledged the salute. "You're an odd sort yourself. That was a vintage Luger in your hand when I intervened. What sort of American tourist carries a prewar pistol?"

The waiter brought my food, and I pitched in. It wouldn't have passed muster in Bangkok, but it tasted fine to me. "It's a long story," I said. "Look, my name's Nickerson. Carter Nickerson." I held out my hand and he shook it. His fist was the size of a small leg of lamb.

"Jean Legras," he said. "Mr. Nickerson: I think you're a cop of some kind. I'm in the trade myself. I can spot another cop when I see one."

I had a feeling about Monsieur Legras. I decided he was all right. "You're right," I told him. "I'm here on a missing persons thing. I'm looking for these girls here. I've traced them this far." I handed over one of the prints I'd had made of the shot of Sandy and Meriem.

"Can't say I've seen them," he said. He polished up the last of his rice with deft movements of the sticks. He was even faster with the sticks than I was. "We're both out of our jurisdiction. I'm an inspector with the Marseilles police. I'm not supposed to do anything official here. But I'm on the trail of something myself, a smuggling ring we drove across the border some months ago. We traced it here. You will have gathered that wasn't hard. Virtually anything off-color—it will wind up here eventually, here where the laws are weak and the taxes all but nonexistent." He tipped up his beer and called for another. "Perhaps we can work in harness. I am staying at *Le Dauphin,* on the *Boulevard du General de Gaulle.*"

"Fine," I said. "You can reach me at the *Splendide.* Room 500."

"Excellent." He stood up. "No, no, finish your lunch. Perhaps we will see one another later? I will keep the photo, if you don't mind. I know places to ask. I come here fairly often in the nature of my work. Perhaps I will give you a call this evening."

"Fine." I stood up to shake his hand; his handshake was even stronger than before. His grin was friendly and tough, an old scrapper's. I sat down and watched him go out, his walk a careless amble. He had a slight limp, very likely from an old war wound, but it didn't slow him down any. One leg was a few millimeters shorter than the other.

Foot traffic in La Condamine picked up by the time I went back out into the street. There was a real glut of tourists out: Germans, Japanese, Danes, Japanese. I had to elbow my way through the crowd.

I picked up another tail almost immediately.

Don't ask me how I knew. I could hardly have told you at any time. It was just a feeling. The crowd was thick enough by now that I couldn't have picked him out anywhere. Well, enough of that. The way to identify a tail is to keep going places where the crowd thins out, a little at a time, until you start noticing the same face wherever you go. I cut up a side street and turned again at the next corner. Then I made my way up an alley and rejoined the first side street again.

The crowd was down to a dozen people or more. I stopped, turned, and watched them. I couldn't see any face I recognized. But the funny thing was, I still felt like somebody being tailed. Whoever he was, he was good. I made my way up the hill, slowly heading for the Casino area. The crowd around me picked up again.

No sign of anybody, but still that same funny feeling I had, localized somewhere around the back of the neck. Ask any pretty woman. She'll know what I'm talking about. Women can tell, blindfolded and with their backs turned, when somebody's staring at their legs. This was that kind of feeling—only there wasn't any pleasant, titillating side to it.

I wasn't just seeing the town, mind you. I had a specific destination in mind. And I sure as hell didn't want anybody tailing me there if I could help it.

AXE had had a contact in Monte Carlo. I hadn't had occasion to use him myself in several years—I hadn't got any closer than Nice, in the Komaroff affair—but I'd had dealings with him in the past.

His name was Conrado Heredia, and he was probably getting on by now. Fifty? Sixty? He could be either. He'd served on the losing side of Franco's civil war forty years ago—but nobody knew how old he was when he'd escaped across the mountains to Andorra in a smuggler's cart, with a price on his head. He'd specialized in explosives then, and this had come in handy later on, when Franco's great and good friend Hitler had taken Paris. He'd been a wizard with everything from nitro to gun cotton, all through the Resistance. After the war he'd enlisted in the *Legion,* like a lot of guys who didn't know any other trade but fighting. Like Jean Legras, he'd seen the bitterest sort of fighting in Vietnam, right up to the day the French lost it.

These days, unless his situation had changed since AXE had gone under, he was supposed to be working as a masseur at the cushiest indoor swimming pool in town, the one that served both the *Hotel de Paris,* on the *Place de Casino,* and the almost equally sumptuous old *Hermitage* on the *Place Beaumarchais.*

Well, what the hell. I could use a massage right now. The side of my neck in particular was stiff as a board. And there probably wasn't a more secure place to have a quiet chat about things best not overheard than the massage rooms of the *Des Terrasses.*

I checked in up front and asked for Monsieur Conrad. The clerk said he'd be right along. And when I sat down I noticed something extremely odd. I *still* had the feeling of being tailed. There wasn't a damn soul there but me. Nevertheless. . . .

I crossed my legs and sat there reading a two-day-old copy of *Le Figaro,* something somebody'd flown in from Paris. Not much was happening in the world that had caught the paper's notice. Six innocent civilians had been blown up by a *plastique* while mailing letters at a rural post office outside the city. An actress had left her husband for another man twenty years younger than she was. Princess Margaret was up to her usual antics. There was trouble brewing in . . .

"Monsieur?"

I looked up. There was a burly man looking down at me. "Yes?" I said. "I'm waiting for *Monsieur* Conrad."

"Eh pardon?" he said. *"Mais, monsieur, je suis Monsieur Conrad."*

The hell he was. I'd never seen him before in my life.

That prickly feeling in the back of my head was getting worse and worse. . . .

I went back to the *Splendide,* feeling like twenty kinds of idiot. But when I checked in at the desk and asked for my key the clerk handed me a handful of messages that had come in. I stuck them in my pocket and headed for the elevator.

And something was still bugging me—that crazy feeling that I wasn't alone, that someone had an eye on me, was watching everything I was doing. . . .

I restrained my curiosity until I'd closed the heavy door of my room behind me. Then I dug the notes out of my pocket.

The first was from Mame in New York: *Will call again at midnight your time.* This one had obviously been transcribed by the clerk in English, on hotel stationery.

The next two that came to hand were both in envelopes with the Splendide logo at the top: the sort of thing you could get from the clerk at the desk if you wanted to leave someone a message. I opened one; it said in French:

M. Nickerson—I think I have found someone who knows something about the missing parties. With your permission I will bring him to your place at ten tonight. Please call me if this is unsatisfactory.—Jean Legras.

Well, I thought, a full evening. That might just give me time to break into the downstairs room beforehand and see what I could find. I stuck a finger under the flap of the other envelope and opened it.

And nearly dropped it.

What is Nick Carter doing in Monte Carlo?

The letter was typed—from the face I'd guess on a German Olympia—and there was no watermark on the otherwise unmarked paper. Well, I thought, there went my cover. I wondered who was trying to be cute, though, and why they'd bother. After all, there were two groups that might have reason, right now, to be curious about my presence here, and either one was likely to know who the hell I was, phony identity or no. Why go around sending me little *billets-doux* like this, anyhow? There was something sophomoric about it all—considering, after all, that we were dealing with people who blew up cars, set people on fire. . . .

The third note was on hotel stationery again, in a hotel envelope.

It was from Angie!

Nick—I'm here, Room 400. We'll be transferred out on the midnight flight from the airport at Nice. We should be leaving about an hour before that. I've got a line on the kids. They're in Zurich. Enroute to where, I don't know—but the word is, they'll still be there when I get there. I'm part of the shipment. I gather they've got somebody big in mind. At least, if you don't come get me I'll wind up in somebody's harem, in an Yvonne De Carlo outfit with a diamond in my belly button—and not in a crib in Bogota banging oilfield workers, 40 a night. Don't let that stop you from sticking your oar in. See you tonight, Angie.

Well, I thought, putting down the letter. A busy evening indeed.

Instinctively I reached up and checked Wilhelmina in her holster. And, feeling that familiar, comforting weight of the old girl as she fairly jumped into my hand, I wondered for perhaps the fiftieth time at the funny feeling I'd had all day, the feeling I couldn't shake even now, in my own room. The feeling that somewhere, somehow, someone was watching everything I did. Watching and listening. . . .

It took until about seven-thirty for the sky outside to get totally dark. Long before then, however, the town had grown gaudy as a carnival midway outside, as bright as Piccadilly or Times Square. Ever wish they hadn't invented neon? I sure did, when I opened my window and looked out and down on the expanse of wall I'd have to be climbing down—and hoping that nobody passing by on the street below had the notion of looking up.

I patted myself down before slipping out onto the sill: Wilhelmina in her holster, Hugo in his sheath up my sleeve, Pierre snug in his pocket down near my lap. It was like a sort of genuflection to whatever gods there were that had kept me alive this far. You go to your church, pal; I'll go to mine.

The rule in Monegasque hotels, even new ones,

is the fifteen-foot ceiling. Thus it was a damn sight farther down at the fifth floor than it might have been in the average building. I looked down once and decided that looking down wasn't where it was at, if you get me. I eased out to where I could shinny down, one finger- or toe-hold at a time, to a point beside that open and well-lit window in Room 400.

Room? It was a suite. It was the kind of joint where the rooms can be converted by unlocking a few doors here and there. I got a quick gander at it as I slipped onto the ledge. It was cushier than mine, roomier.

I stuck my head a little farther out and looked around. There was a big, heavyset man—maybe my height or so and fifty musclebound pounds heavier—standing by the big fourposter bed. Looking down.

Angie Negri was on her knees, naked, before him. There were bruises all over that pretty face. Her hands were shackled to the bed. She was looking up at him with an expression of utter loathing in her dark eyes. He was doing something to the front of his pants. . . .

I slipped all the way onto the sill. Nobody had spotted me so far. Now I could hear what they were saying:

"Goddam you, Claude," Angie said. "Don't you even try it. So help me God in heaven, I'll ruin you. I'll bite the thing off. I'll—"

"I could crush your skull between these hands, you know. It would be so easy—"

"Look, for the love of Christ, unlock my hands. Look, I can make you feel good. I can make you feel a damn sight better if you play ball with me and get this hardware off me than you could ever possibly feel raping me. I'll make it terrible for you if you force me. If you don't . . . if you treat me right. . . ."

"Hmmm. . . . Well, perhaps. . . ."

I slipped down to the floor right about then. She saw me immediately. She made a face: *quiet there now.* I knew what she wanted. She wanted to get those hands free first. I nodded and moved slowly toward them on tiptoe.

"There," she said, "that's better, baby, now just you come here and. . . ." I could see her hand now; the cuffs were off.

Naked little Angie went into action like Billy Jack. As a movie, it would have been halfway between porno and a Bruce Lee movie. She gave him a straight shot to the pills, did a backflip to land half-erect on those little bare feet, and attacked. Two hand feints and a swinging flying kick that nearly took the big man's head off—a wild chop at his neck and bedamned if he didn't go straight over and down like a felled tree. The fall must have broken his nose all by itself.

She stood up, rubbing her wrists. Her eyes flashed. "Excuse me, Nick," she said. "I forgot to dress for company." She brushed herself off, dismissing him with a glance—and looked up to catch me grinning. Or leering. I honestly couldn't tell you which.

"Well, thanks," she said. "I mean, for coming to rescue the fair maiden. Thanks even more for letting *me* clobber the son of a bitch."

"My pleasure," I said. I swear to God, she was the sexiest sight I'd seen in a month of Sundays, all naked and full of electricity like that. "I'll spare you the cliché about how beautiful you look when you're mad."

"Don't spare me," she said, looking around for her clothes. "Nick, you tell me that as often as you like. Right now, my ego's in lousy shape. This bastard and . . . and the other one . . . they drugged me and raped me about an hour after I wrote you that note and sent it down by messenger." She found her pants suit and was about to slip into it when I reached for her and pulled her to me. I kissed her hard, then soft, then hard. . . .

"Mmmmm," she said. "Remind me to continue this later, Nicky. Upstairs. Right now we gotta get out of here." She hugged me once, quick, and got into the pants suit. "My suitcase's over there," she said. "Now quick. Let's do something about Buster here. Hey, wait." She fiddled in a drawer and came out with a hypodermic and a bottle of something. "Look. Here's the crap they mickeyed me with. I'm gonna put Roscoe here out of commission for another twenty-four hours or so. A double dose of this crap ought to do it. . . ." She suited action to word. He didn't even move as she slipped the needle in his arm.

Then she looked up at me. "Okay," she said. "The main thing is we gotta make tracks. You're gonna replace Claude on that midnight shipment to Zurich, Nick. It's the only thing that makes any sense at all. They don't know him there, and I know all the password junk. I only wish we had time to wait for the other one and knock him off too. Well, those are the breaks. Let's go. No, hand me my shoes there. I'll put 'em on when we're the hell out of here."

I couldn't resist giving her one more hug. Then I

picked her up—tough as she was, she was light as a feather, and soft all the places a girl's supposed to be soft—and set her on the windowsill. "Upsy daisy," I said.

THIRTEEN

I went up the wall carefully. She went up like a monkey, surefooted, surefingered, as if a drop of ninety feet or so were nothing to worry about. When I got to the window she was sitting on the sill offering me a hand up, a big grin on that cute face.

"Thanks," I said, throwing my legs up and over. I handed her down, more out of gallantry than anything. She sure as hell didn't need anything from my helping hand—unless the thing she needed was something to prop up an ego that had been badly eroded in the last twenty-four hours.

Well, I could do something about that. I grabbed her and slowly unbuttoned her blouse, revealing her lush, dark-nippled breasts. In two shakes she had skinned out of everything. . . .

In a while I sent for brandy. Somebody delivered a bottle of Remy Martin and two glasses. I also asked for the check and the bellboy said he'd bring it up. I poured us two snifters and took a delicious sniff of mine before drinking it.

She'd wandered over to the mirror and was looking herself over with horror. "Oh, Nicky, I look an absolute mess. Why didn't you tell me? My God, I've got to do something about this. . . ."

"Tell you about what?" I said. "You look terrific to me, pal." She did, too. She still hadn't put on a stitch. I was reminding myself to take her somewhere on vacation, soon as we had this job in the can, where she didn't have to dress. I could look at Angie in the buff all day and not get tired. Well . . . I might get tired at the end of the day, but it wouldn't be from looking.

"Thanks, Nick. Keep it up. My ego's doing a lot better after that, baby, but keep up the soft soap. I can use all of it that I can get. In the meantime I have to do something about this hair."

"Okay," I said. "I'll run a tub . . . huh. Look at that, a real shower, American style." You'd never find that at one of the Old Guard places. "I'll run you some hot water, okay? There's some shampoo in my bag. . . ."

"Thanks, Nicky. You're a doll." When the water was right she skipped past me, stopping for a quick kiss, and got into the shower amid huge clouds of steam. I went out and closed the bathroom door behind me.

There was another knock on the door. The porter? I brought my brandy glass along . . . and as I raised my arm to drink I caught a glimpse of my watch. Ten p.m.! How time did fly. . . .

I opened the door. Legras stood there, with a tough *apache* type he'd dragged in from the street. I looked the new guy over. He was about six-two and well over two hundred. "Hello," I said. I shook hands with both of them, showing them in. "Here," I said. "Brandy?"

"No, no," Legras said, smiling. The two of them sat down on the daybed. "Mr. Nickerson, this is Achille Sardou. He does not speak English. He is a smuggler, dealing in cigarettes, alcoholic beverages, cocaine—mainly small stuff except for the cocaine. And he's too small-time to get much of that kind of traffic. Last week he did some work for a group that operates both out of here and out of Marseilles—which is where I got to know him."

"What kind of group?" I said.

"There is a ring which kidnaps young girls, you know, and forcibly recruits them for the brothels of Algeria, Morocco, Egypt."

"That's what I'm afraid happened to the two chicks I told you about."

"My point exactly. He was the driver on a—what is the American term? Is it 'milk run'? Anyway, he was ferrying a busload of young recruits to Monaco for dispersal. They thought they were coming here on an excursion. Once here, their 'chaperon' would drug them and have them turned over to the dregs of the night world here for multiple rape. The idea is to destroy, in as short a time as possible, all trace of pride, of self-respect, to convince the girls that they are once and for all beyond escape, beyond redemption. And of course, as they perform while drugged, copious amounts of photographs are taken. The idea is to blackmail them by telling them their parents, their friends, their home town newspapers would receive copies of the pictures if they did not cooperate in the next phase. . . ."

"And this ox here?" I shot the big moose a contemptuous glance. "He thinks the girls were part of the shipment?"

"Yes," Legras said. "I have pumped him for what I could get out of him. He is going back with me to France. I have offered him a reduced sentence for a lesser crime than kidnapping if he testifies. I think I can break up at least the Marseilles checkpoint in this ring. He knows that if he does not testify—if he does not, in a word, sing like a cuckoo—I will take action against his wife and child."

"What'll you do?"

"I will sell her into the whorehouse of a rival band. I will put the child in a workhouse. This business is not play, Mr. Nickerson. I want this traffic stopped."

"He thinks he saw them?"

"Yes. The one with the red hair and the one who looks like an *Algerienne*. They seem to be held somewhat apart by the gang. They were not raped along with the rest, so far as Sardou knows. This *cochon* participated in the rapes. He knows which ones were the victims. There is something special about those two, though. They were held separately in a house here in the Principality. The destination, I believe, was Zurich. The *first* destination, at any rate."

"That checks out with other information I've received," I said. "Look. This Sardou. He'll be going directly to jail in France? He won't get a chance to contact any of his gang?"

"*Mais non.* And he knows better than to attack me and escape. He knows my assistant in Marseilles has instructions to go ahead with our plans for his family if there is the smallest hitch in our schedule."

"Good. There's somebody I'd like to have talk to him for a moment. If you'll wait a moment?"

I went to the bathroom door and opened it a crack. She was inside toweling down, her hair pinned up, looking pink and adorable. "Angie," I said. "My French cop is outside, and he's got one of the couriers that brought Sandy and Meriem in from Marseilles. I thought you might want to pump him some before the French sneak him back across the border and drop him in the slam."

"Okay," she said. "I'll borrow your robe. . . ." She dug it out of my bag and slipped it on. "Just let me straighten my hair a bit, I look like the Wicked Witch of the West."

I came back out into the room. Legras and the *apache* type were standing. Legras was watching Sardou's big meaty hands; his own scarred right hand was conveniently close to his lapel, and I could see the bulge of a pistol under there. He wasn't taking any chances. Looking Sardou over—tall, rangy, with heavy shoulders and basketball-player hands, a mean glint in his eye—I could see why. Legras was tough, but not tough enough to take somebody like this without the kind of help a heavy pistol gives you. "She'll be right out," I said.

"Fine," Legras said. His eye was on the big man. He was prepared for the eventuality that Angie would recognize the *apache* and put up a holler—and that Sardou would react. I figured he knew his man. Now, as I watched, he growled a warning at the big man in a gruff *Marseillais* argot. I didn't catch one word in three. All he got as answer was a grudging grunt.

The door behind me opened. "Angie," I said, "this is Inspector Legras of the Marseilles police, and that scum with him is. . . ."

"Nick."

I turned to look at her. She looked cute as ever in my big robe, her little brown feet poking out from below the bottom seam. Her eyes were filled with horror.

"Yeah, honey?" I said. "Is that the one?"

Her voice changed. "Nick. . . ." It was plaintive, despairing. Her little hand pointed ineffectually back at the two of them.

I whirled.

Legras's gun was out. And it was pointing at me. There was no humor in his eyes at all. And the big *apache* was advancing on me.

And now he looked at her. "Ah," he said. "We thought we might find you here. It was, however, not worth flushing our Mr. 'Nickerson' "—the way he pronounced the word I knew he was on to me, and had been from the first—"unless we were sure."

"Nick," Angie said. *"He's* the one. He's the . . . the other one I told you about. The one that raped me. . . ."

"I see," I said. "Legras and not Sardou." I backed off toward the corner, away from Angie. The farther I could separate the pair of us, the better. "Angie," I said, "between 'em they've only got one gun."

"Got you," she said.

"Stay where you are," Legras barked. "Sardou —get Carter." I looked at Legras's face, with its smirk of superiority, and then back at the big ox advancing on me. Then I caught a quick motion of Legras's hand as Angie moved farther toward the far wall.

I moved—and fast.

One hand went inside the other arm's sleeve. In a split blink Hugo—razor-sharp, perfectly balanced Hugo—was in my hand. I flipped him in a perfect one-and-a-half. He went into Legras's arm, right on target, all the way across the room. I didn't stop to look at what happened. The big ox was on me. My hand went back inside my jacket, and I had Wilhelmina out and half-cocked when he hit me. I just had time, turning, to see the heavy ashtray in his hand as he slugged me with it. That was all, baby.

I woke up with a hell of a headache.

The room was empty. There were a few bloodstains near the couch, on the rug.

I went in the bathroom. Angie's clothes were gone. My suitcase had been ripped to shreds.

I looked at my watch. Eleven-thirty. They'd be on the boarding dock now, at the Nice airport, ready for the flight out to Zurich.

They had Angie. And now they knew the whole thing. They knew who it was we were looking for, and what Angie's involvement was. And they were sending her to her death.

And the goddam phone was ringing, ringing. . . .

FOURTEEN

I poured myself a glass of brandy. At least they'd left me that. Then I picked up the telephone.

"Your call from New York," the desk man said.

"Okay." I took a slug of the brandy. Never mind that you're not supposed to take brandy by the slug. I would have socked it down if it'd been straight hemlock, with no chaser.

There was surprisingly little static. "Hello? Nick? It's Mame."

"Hi baby. What have you got?"

"You don't sound glad to hear from me. What's the matter?"

"I found Angie, and I got her away from them . . . but they took her back. I've got a lump on my head the size of a bowling ball and she's on her way to Zurich on the midnight plane."

"Matt Keller's on vacation in Lucerne. Nick—maybe we can get him to meet the plane and tail them." She gave me his address and number.

"What else have you got for me?"

"Everything's under control. Somebody took a potshot at Mike Willis in Aspen, up on the slopes. He tracked the guy down, busted his neck, and dropped him down a crevasse and kicked some snow down on top of him. Not bad work for a guy with a .38 slug in one arm."

"Does he know who it was?"

"Little Japanese guy. Tough as bloody hell. He had a tattoo on his right hand, between the thumb and the forefinger. It was a Sino-Japanese ideogram, and it looked like a teeter-totter. A little inverted V with a straight line balanced atop it. He. . . ."

"Mame. Give him a fifty-buck bonus or something. Hug him. Let him cop a feel or whatever you can think of. He's earned it."

"I don't get it. I'll figure out some way of rewarding him"—her voice sounded randy all the way from the U.S.—"but I still don't get it."

"Get out your Roget's. What free-associates from *teeter-totter,* anyhow?"

"Uh . . . seesaw, lever, fulcrum, pivot—" She stopped. "*Nick.*"

"Right on, sugar. Tip off all the boys. And call Barker at the Bureau. Ask him what the ideogram means."

"Got you. Nick: was Angie . . . okay?"

"When I left her. I make no guarantees. She'd been raped and she was mad as hell. I watched her demolish one of 'em barehanded, a guy a foot taller than she was. If anybody could come out of this alive and in one piece, she could. . . ."

"But?" She caught the nuance in my voice.

"But . . . I'm crossing my fingers."

"Me too. You go get her. And call Matt Keller.

Right away. Tell him to get on the stick."

"Right, baby. Keep up the good work."

"Take care, Nick." When I hung up my headache was already a little better. I took another slug of brandy and put a call into Keller.

I threw my goddam suitcase down the disposal chute on the way out the door. I paid up and asked the night man to call me a cab. I was feeling a little better—physically—but I was in a bad humor that even finishing the bottle of Remy Martin hadn't been able to cure.

I was in such a punk frame of mind that it took all the way out to the cab stand for me to get that funny feeling of being watched again. I looked around. Nobody there but the porter, and even he was slipping back inside now in the night chill. There was a lot of transplanted greenery around the front of the hotel, and if somebody were watching me there was a lot of room behind all those bushes for him to hide in.

The desk man had said the cab would be a few minutes. I decided to get a little closer to all that convenient greenery. As I did one hand crept close to my lapel, where Wilhelmina still hung in her oiled holster.

"All right," I said. "Whoever you are. Come out and let's have a little chat." I listened, walking slowly around the bushes. Nothing. I repeated approximately the same in French and Italian. Neither language worked. I tried German, with the same kind of results. Russian. Spanish.

There was a little rustle in the bushes. I reached in my pocket and pulled out one of those dollar flashlights, the throwaway kind. I moved cautiously down next to a pair of cypresses, standing tall near the doorway.

The rustle sounded again.

I crept forward—I was totally out of the light by now, and it was pitch dark—and suddenly shone the little light on the place the noise had come from.

There was a man down there. He seemed to be trying to say something—but as I shone the little light full on him I could see why he couldn't. Somebody'd cut his throat, and recently, and he was dying from it. He couldn't do much other than gurgle.

I knelt beside him, the light still on him. His face was swarthy, big-nosed, a Middle Eastern kind of face. He tried to talk again.

"Don't try, pal. You'll just go out hurting. Look. Who was it got you? Was it Legras? Sardou? Move your hand counterclockwise if it was."

His hand moved—weakly, but unmistakeably.

"Who are you? Are you after them too?"

His hand didn't move. But as I looked close I could see that his hand wasn't ever going to move again. That weak spark had gone out, permanently. I turned the light off. . . .

. . . And then I turned it back on again.

I picked up his right hand. No ideogram. There was nothing on his left either. I was just about to douse the light and get the hell out of there when I looked at his wrist.

There was something odd about his watch.

I pulled it off his unresisting hand and stuck it in the light. I turned it over. And then—I was breathing hard by now—I stuck it in my pocket. I reached inside his jacket pocket and yanked his wallet and a morocco-bound notebook.

I patted all the places people usually carry pockets and found nothing except the bulge of a small revolver in his hip pocket. I stashed the wallet and the notebook in my coat.

Then I stood up and moved out into the light again—just in time for the cab to pull up in the driveway. I opened the door and got in. "Airport," I said.

Once on the road I got out the little flash again and turned it on. I went through the wallet first. It identified him as Fuad Amirsolaimani, a citizen of Egypt. There were the usual credit cards everyone has these days. There were a few scraps of paper with squiggles in Arabic on them. I couldn't make out a damn bit of it.

The same with the notebook. The only thing that caught my eye that I could make head or tail of—all the rest was in Arabic, and what I took to be an exceptionally sloppy variety of Arabic at that—was the little logo stamped on the inside front cover. It looked like this:

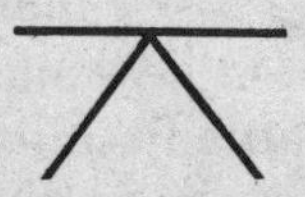

Well, maybe there was another meaning. Maybe there was another interpretation. Maybe I was full of malarkey. Maybe the little logo spelled "April Fool" in Chinese or Japanese or whatever. Maybe it was a picture of a table, or a picture of Danton after the guillotine hit him. But until I had a better explanation I was willing to bet it had something to do with Code Name Pivot. But if it was—how had this guy come by it, if (and this was a damned big if) he wasn't one of the gang? At least that was the way I read the fact that I hadn't found any teeter-totter logo on his hands.

More questions.

What was he doing here? Trying to kill me? Trying to warn me? Or was it all just a matter of coincidence?

I discounted the latter immediately.

For one thing, it was just laying on too goddam thick for me to believe I'd quite coincidentally run across somebody who'd just had his throat cut by Legras and his *apache* buddy—and find out he was carrying a notebook bearing the logo of a group that had been trying to eliminate not only me, but others in my organization. All of whom had worked for the same governmental Department of Dirty Tricks back in those dear bygone days before Admiral What's-His-Face.

No. Nuts. Phooey. It smelled to high heaven. He'd been trying to reach me, all right—but whether to do me some goodies or some baddies was a matter I couldn't say right now.

Besides, there was that goddam watch I'd taken off him. I pulled it out now and looked at it under the light from the little flash.

It was a good watch, an Omega, but the case wasn't anything special. The owner was the kind of guy who liked things that worked, but didn't give a good goddam if they were wrapped fancy. The case wasn't gold; it was stainless steel, the kind they don't export from the firm. The band was one of these two-dollar things you buy in the neighborhood drug store.

It was a good watch. Ten years old and still keeping good time.

I knew the watch well. It belonged to David Hawk.

I'd asked Matt to call ahead for me and land me a flop at the airport hotel, north of Zurich at Glattbrug. I needed forty winks before doing anything. He'd said sure; he'd leave me a message at the desk.

On the flight I had time to consider my situation. Where had the dying man in La Condamine got that watch? Had he taken it off David's body—or had David given it to him for some reason?

Hawk? Dead? Another victim of the Code Word Pivot crowd?

FIFTEEN

Matt was waiting for me as I came down the ramp. In our trade they don't run to pretty. The one thing you notice, if you ever meet anybody who used to work for AXE or for any other comparable outfit is that the features tend to be regularish but nothing special. We can turn it off, all of us, and disappear into the woodwork until you can walk right by us, standing there in the open air, and not notice us. Me? You might like the way I looked if I wanted you to—and if I turned on the Carter charm. But I can turn it off too. I had to learn to. It's why I'm still alive and able to talk about it all.

Matt Keller was smaller than most, about five-seven or so. The features had been regular once, and then three guys had gone to work on him in an alley after, not before, somebody had sapped him one. Now his nose listed to starboard a bit, and the brows were lumpy, and he looked like an intelligent stevedore, and he talked low and raspy. Three years later somebody had cut his throat and left him to die, and while Matt had got some satisfaction out of zapping his assailant something like ten days after the hospital'd let him go, it was too late to do his tonsils any good. He might find some satisfactions in life afterward, but matching high notes with Luciano Pavarotti wouldn't be one of 'em.

He looked down at my empty right hand as I approached. "No suitcase?" he said. He had a toothpick in his face as usual. I wondered where he'd gotten any in Zurich. They don't use 'em in Europe much.

"What do I need with a suitcase?" I said. I fell into step with him. "So what have you got?"

"I know where they are, if that's what you want."

"Great," I said. "And Angie? Do you know anything about Angie?"

"The cute little Italian dish? She's one of ours?"

"Yeah. And she's as good an op as you are, pal. But she's our inside man, if you'll pardon the term. And her cover's blown."

Keller whistled long and low. There was the authentic tone of chagrin in that whistle. "Wow. When they brought her in she was stoned. Drunk as a skunk."

"Drugged," I said. "Damn. Look, Matt. She's in deep trouble. We've gotta get her out—and without alerting these types she came in with to what we're up to. Now they know me by sight, and they know who I am."

"Balls," Matt said. "It was shaping up as a nice vacation."

I was halfway through the business of bringing

him up to date over lunch and a couple of beers when he stopped me dead. "Code Name Pivot?" he said, his eyes lighting up. "Nick, I was on that one. That was who cut my neck for me."

I put down my knife and fork and looked at him. "For God's sake. I thought it was one of those things nobody left alive but Hawk knew about." I frowned. "I'm assuming Hawk's alive."

"Hawk?" Matt's expression was contemptuous. "The day ain't dawned when they can get that tough old bastard. You couldn't kill Hawk ramming a stick of dynamite up his ass and lighting it. You couldn't feed him to Godzilla. Hell, Nick, Hawk ain't even gonna die of old age. He'll be around when the rest of us have been replaced by robots."

"I hope you're right," I said. "Tell me about Code Name Pivot."

He did. I'll boil it down for you, the little Hawk had told Matt before the guys with the knives had got to him. "Pivot" meant, of course, balance of power. The outfit was something calling itself Bloody Thursday, after the day it pulled off its first big bombing. The group was international, ostensibly terrorist in outline but mercenary in spirit. They actually rented out terror squads—bombers, kidnappers, assassins, arsonists—to a wide variety of international pressure groups who had axes to grind—but who found it more profitable as well as better publicity if they paid for having their work done by middle men. They'd killed Hammarskjold for one side in the Congo war, for instance, and then come right back and assassinated Lumumba for the other.

And then Hawk had caught on to them. And

Hawk, telling only the operatives involved, had moved in on them, put them under surveillance, and put a crimp in their style. And Matt had been the first op to lock horns with them—to his loss. They'd killed Mickey Henderson shortly after that, and Les Quincannon. And then Hawk had taken a month off and blown up their headquarters in Paris himself.

I knew he wasn't the type to sit his whole life behind a desk. Hell, before I was out of short pants David had been the greatest op the Feds had ever had outside the country. Tough, resourceful, brilliant. And deadly. Enough of his contemporaries—wonderful old Will Lockwood back in Hong Kong, for instance—had told me of Hawk's youthful exploits to convince me he had been the deadliest of them all. And I'd worked in harness with him, even fairly recently, and knew what an op he still was the moment circumstances forced him out from behind that desk.

But this? Hawk going on vacation and, single-handed, taking on an entire terrorist organization and putting them—however temporarily—out of commission like that? This was a side of Hawk that surprised me. And cheered me, and gave me hope. After all, it increased the possibility that my worst fears—that this Pivot crowd, which somehow had got hold of Hawk's favorite wristwatch, had somehow managed to get to him and put him away.

"Finish your chow. Meanwhile," Matt said now, "here's what's happening. The cute little piece of pasta—Angie? Nice name—got stuck in a taxi and taken over to someplace on Lake Zurich. She's there now. I got somebody on the case, a nice tough Schwyzer op that I worked with some years ago. Old friend. I got a number I can call for info every so often, and whenever I move I leave the new number for my friend to call in. They could have plans to bump her off. My friend's on to that, Nick. With orders to intervene only if it gets down to that kind of jazz before we get there. But the main thing is not to disturb things until we can find out where the hell they've taken the two chicks we're here to find in the first place. Right?"

"Right. I should have known you were on top of things." I finished my beer. "Do you know anything about the agenda? About where they've taken the kids?"

He reached inside his jacket and pulled out some sheets of paper, folded three ways the way newspapermen fold copy paper for making notes. He looked the top sheet over. "Listen," he said. "Angie's in a big house overlooking the Lake, like I said. Reason they're there is they're waiting for an emissary from the Big Cheese. The guy they're going to sell the kids to."

"Sounds like you know who the Big Cheese is."

"No," Matt said, "I don't know. But whoever the hell he is, he draws an uncommon lot of water, let me tell you. And what we've got so far, what with the necessity of using quickie equipment to wiretap the bastards, is that he's over in Graubünden—Canton Grisons. He's got some sort of cushy layout up in the hills above Chur, way I understand it, and the damn thing's laid out like a fortress. Who he is—well, we're not sure, but I've got the worst kind of feelings. The one chick . . . you said she was the daughter of this Sheikh what's his name?"

"Yeah."

"Okay. Well, my partner looked him up. He's got enemies. People who want him and his moderate ways the hell out of the way. They've tried to get to him time and time again. It's never worked, because he's a pretty tough cookie. And his own personal staff of guards is as mean and competent as that Israeli gang that made the raid on Entebbe. Having failed to get to him directly—"

"They got his daughter. Yeah. Meriem was at the school under a phony name, and a lot of trouble had been gone to to make sure nobody knew whose kid she was. I get you. You mean it's a blackmail thing?"

"Well, maybe. I sure as hell hope so. I mean, if it's blackmail there's a chance that they'll leave the kid alone long enough to collect some dough on her. I mean, she might live through it all. Whether she'll stay a virgin long—or whether she's still one, for that matter—well, that's up to the Man Upstairs."

"So, the way I see it," I said, "the question's this: do we want to just run in there and rescue 'em? Or do we want to break this thing up too? This kidnap-the-chicks-and-sell-'em-into-slavery crap?" We both knew the answer to that. I went on. "I'm a creature of habit. But what it'll mean is breaking this operation into two pieces. One of us will have to mastermind the completion of it. The other one will have to kidnap the two kids away from 'em, once we've established who it is we're dealing with, and skedaddle for home. Remember, there's a deadline still. Okay?"

"Okay with me, buddy." His shrug showed how poorly his jacket fit him. He looked loose and shambling and no more than halfway put together.

But I knew better. A camel looks like something some drunken sculptor put together when he was so shit-faced he couldn't see straight, much less stand up. No matter. Put him in his own element and the camel will outlast anybody or anything, and laugh at you as you die. Same way with Matt.

"Flip you for which job."

"We'll see." I shoved some dough under the bill and got up. "Come on, let's get the hell out of here."

"Wait," he said. "Gotta call my contact. I got a car waiting outside for us. Give me three minutes." He waved and disappeared into the back of the restaurant, where a row of *Fernsprecher* equipment stood just outside the bathrooms.

I looked back toward the phones. Matt was slumped against the wall, one bony elbow holding him up. He had the phone receiver tucked behind his ear. He looked like a puppet at rest. Good man, I was thinking.

And then the sixth sense kicked me in the ass hard.

Something was wrong. Matt hadn't moved in—how long?

I pushed my way back through the crowd to the rank of phones. The moment I touched his back with one exploratory hand his body just sort of crumpled to the floor. The phone hung dangling above him.

And I could see the little red hole where somebody'd stuck a silenced small-bore pistol against his head, right above one ear, and blown his brains all over the wall.

SIXTEEN

The pay phone next to his rang.

I looked around. Nobody had spotted anything yet. I picked up the phone. "Hello?" I said.

"Herr Keller, bitte?" The voice was a woman's, and the accent was purest Mittel-Europa.

"He's not here," I said. "This is Nick Carter, his boss. Who am I talking to?"

There was a pause on the other end. "I . . . my name is Heitmeyer. Traudl Heitmeyer. Herr . . . ah . . . Mr. Carter. Is something wrong?" The voice was concerned, but controlled.

"Yeah, there is. I bet you've got some news for me, but for God's sake let's hold it. Is there a number I can call you back at, a few minutes from now?"

"Yes." She gave it to me. It was a long-distance number. "Please. It is important. Call me as soon as possible." She hung up.

So did I. And I chanced to look down at my feet, where Matt Keller was sleeping his last sleep. He was almost between my legs. Looking down at him meant moving my head a trifle.

Doing so saved my life. If I hadn't looked down . . . well, maybe Mame Ferguson would be telling this story and not me, right about now.

The gun said *phut* and spat something at me from behind my head. The bullet creased my cheek and plowed into the wall. I wheeled and saw a man in a brown coat shouldering his way through the crowd. "Hey!" I bellowed, throwing caution to the winds. "Stop that man! Murder! Stop that man! He's just killed someone!"

But the Swiss aren't any better at getting in the way of an armed murderer than Americans are. The effect was to make everyone draw away from him, the more so since he was waving that silencer-equipped pistol around. I thought of drawing Wilhelmina and throwing down on him myself, but there were too many damn civilians in the way.

I was nearly an hour with the cops before I got free to make a phone call. By that time I'd given them a few security numbers—I still had a few friends in the right places in the Swiss government—and had them off my own neck. I also had a nice little scar on my face, neatly bandaged.

I was also seething with ice-cold rage.

They gave me a room with a phone. I rejected it and went next door to a pay phone, and wound up in a terrific hassle just getting the change to call with. By the time I finally got through a full hour had passed.

"Es sprecht Frau Heitmeyer."

"Hello," I said. "Nick Carter here."

"Oh, thank God! I was beginning to—please, Mr. Carter. What happened? Mr. Keller—"

"Matt's dead. Somebody got to him just as he was getting ready to call you. In a way you're lucky. He hadn't had time to dial. If he had somebody might have got your number, watching over his shoulder as he dialed."

"Oh, God. No."

"Yeah. I'm mad as hell. When my mad wears down I'm going to have time to be sad as hell. Matt was a good man, one of the very best. Now, tell me: Who are you?"

"I . . . Matt and I were . . . lovers once. We worked together on a case before. For AXE. David Hawk got the recommendation from Kurt Brenner of Interpol's Berne office."

"I see. You want a job? Matt was working for me. I need. . . ."

"Mr. Carter. I would work for nothing. Matt and I. . . . We had begun to . . . well, things were getting together for us again. When I knew him before I was married. What could have been a very fine love affair came to nothing . . . or not very much anyway. Now, with my husband dead. . . ." She made a sound that could have been a rigidly repressed sob, but got herself under control again. "Yes, I will take the job. Matt told me a little about it."

"Okay. Then all you gotta do is tell me what's up, and where to come."

"Yes." She gave me directions to the place, quickly and competently. "Now," she said. "The time is two p.m. If you rent a car it will take you a little under an hour. This will be all right. The contact man does not arrive until around four. If there is agreement he will take them to the person whom he represents. This will take them through Chur, say, around nightfall. The trip to the house where delivery will be made will take a trifle longer, I think. The road is uphill, and is an old one, with many curves—I cannot think of the word."

"Switchbacks? S curves?"

"Yes. A dangerous road. The more so since we, following them up it, will have to drive it without lights."

"Any other complications I ought to know about?"

"No. Well, yes. Dress warmly. It gets cold in Graubünden nights. And there will be some climbing. Wear proper clothing for this."

"Check." I hung up. I sure as hell was trusting a lot to a pleasant voice on the phone that I'd never heard before.

I rented a big black Mercedes, about five years old: stodgy and reliable. I'd picked up a few tools on the way and stowed them in the back seat along with a black sweater and some rubber slippers, the kind you pull on over your shoes. I'd brought some of the latter for her too.

The view along the lake is nice if you like lakes. Personally I've always thought Zurich dull, and the nice part of Switzerland, for me, is the part that goes up and down rapidly. Still and all, the area I'd reached by the time Traudl Heitmeyer's directions had begun to fit the territory was pretty nice, and when I pulled off the road and parked the car in a grove of trees I could smell the fresh air and feel the nice breeze off the lake. Looking toward Zurich you could see the standard temperature inversion they have over every damn city in the world, but in any other direction it was free and clear.

It was a nice location for the big house on top of the hill, all right. There was a thick grove of trees between me and it, and I couldn't see a thing; but I'd caught a glimpse of it from the road. It had a high wall and outbuildings. It was big as hell, with wings to the side. Stretching the point a trifle, the way they do in not-quite-egalitarian postwar Bavaria, you might have called it a *Schloss*. Well, it would have done justice to a count or a baron, I thought, and one who hadn't fallen on evil days either.

Getting there was no problem most of the way. The grove gave me cover almost all of the way to that high wall; but the wall itself was going to prove formidable. Not only was it a nice tall one: you'd be totally exposed going over it. This, I was thinking as I jogged lightly up the hill under those trees, could never be what Traudl Heitmeyer had been talking about when she'd mentioned that some climbing lay ahead.

At the foot of that high barrier I was looking it over, wondering what the hell to do, when I heard a *Psssst!* at my side. I wheeled, Wilhelmina already in my hand—and found myself staring into the biggest, loveliest blue eyes in Switzerland.

She was tall, athletic, a Diana Rigg type—except for that face. The face was irregular, warm, wonderful, vulnerable. The mouth was wide and generous and eminently kissable, even occupied as it was with shushing me. The eyes were large and ocean-blue—and hurt. "Mr. Carter," she said softly.

"Traudl," I said. The two of us ducked under a projection on the wall and looked around us before looking at each other. "I've been trying to figure out how the hell to get in. I think this is one of those occasions when it won't do to pay your way in at the door."

"Correct," she said, and squeezed my hand. There was something electric just in that touch, and her hand felt soft and cool and competent: the hand of a man's woman, but one who wasn't clingy or dependent. It felt good. I squeezed back and continued holding it. "However," she said, "I *have* been busy. If you come around this way the groundskeeper's cottage is outside the wall. This was where Matt—" She choked on the word and couldn't go on for a moment.

"Look," I said, "you'll want to know this. They got him at the telephone, just as he was getting ready to call you. His last thought was of you. I can all but guarantee that."

She had herself under control now, though. "Yes. Yes, he would be that way. And thank you for saying this. But come." And she dragged me by the hand a few steps before letting go and leading the way. From the rear she was every bit as lovely as from the front, in her formfitting black sweater and trim ski pants that showed off her adorable dancer's behind to wonderful advantage. I looked down and noted she was wearing black sneakers: good girl.

The groundskeeper's cottage had a deserted look about it, but after we got inside I could see that she and Matt had cleaned it up a bit and made themselves a nice workspace, with room for the radio equipment and even a single three-quarter bed with an eiderdown coverlet. "Here," she said when the door was secure. "This will be relatively safe. The wind is generally off the lake, and the dogs cannot pick up any trace of scent from here." She motioned to me to sit down in front of a stack of modular radio equipment.

"This is your tapping stuff?" I said.

"Yes. And the 'telephone' you called me back on. There had once been a jack here for the groundskeeper, but he was fired and not replaced some time back, I understand. Matt reactivated it and plugged in. That radio there is the telephone tap for the big house; the other is a multiple room tap. I put those in myself, posing as an electrical inspector. You can have your choice of four rooms in the house. It is highly likely that the kidnappers are meeting with their contact right about now. I saw his car come up perhaps fifteen minutes before you. He was early. I think the discussion ought to take place in the library: that will be position number four on your dial there."

I switched it on. There was no sound. I tried the three other positions. No soap quite yet. I switched them off for now and looked at her. "You've done a terrific job. Matt said you were a hell of an operative."

"He was gallant. I do what I can." She lit a Gauloise bleue and held the pack out to me. I took one and lit up. We sat watching each other through the curling smoke. Just for precaution I cut the radio back on, and left it at setting number four—but turned way down.

"You're brave as hell," I said. "I think you may well be the bravest woman I've ever met. No, I don't mean all this. Lots of people can play at the derring-do game, including a lot of cowards both male and female. But you . . . you're feeling desolate and empty and lost and alone and the one thing in the world you want most is to just come apart and have a good cry, and maybe holler and break things. . . . And here you are calmly discussing wiretap technicalities. Lady, my hat's off to you. Permanently."

"Mr. Carter . . . Nick," she said. "You have no idea how close to the brink I am right now. If I relax this self-control for so much as a moment—" She took another deep draught of the cigarette and sent blue smoke into the air, her eyes still on me, large and liquid and on the verge of tears. "Nick—would you do something for me? Just as a favor from one comrade to another? One colleague to another?"

"I'm at your command," I said.

"Please . . . make love to me now. Quickly. I need—I need—"

She didn't have to finish the sentence. She looked into my eyes and put out her cigarette. I put out mine. She kicked off the sneakers, her eyes still on mine, and skinned down her pants and stepped out of them. Now she stood before me still wearing the sweater and nothing else. The pants were all she took off. She looked nakeder that way than she could ever have done in the altogether: nakeder, more womanly, more vulnerable, more irresistible. Her belly was flat and soft; her thighs were smooth and tapering; her legs were sensationally delicate and beautiful; her *ecu,* covered with lush curling blonde hair. . . .

"Nick, please." She stepped into my arms, her lips raised to meet mine. She hugged me hard, her eyes streaming with tears, and her strong little hand went down to feel the quick hardening of my own flesh and unzip me. . . . "Nick. Here on the bed. We have only moments, moments. . . ."

* * *

I have to say this for them. They were damn polite about their timing. She stifled her dark moans of pleasure, biting hard into the eiderdown, and kept things miraculously quiet, considering her natural inclination was to scream bloody murder and wake the neighborhood. As I plowed into her, keeping my mind somehow on business, I reminded myself to try the whole business again sometime soon, this time with candles, fine wine and soft music. This was a lady you somehow wanted to travel first class with.

So things went quietly, despite all that spur-of-the-moment passion her desperation and loneliness had brought on. I could listen for sounds on the monitor. And glory be, the action didn't move over to the library, over at the big house atop the hill, until a moment or two after she'd convulsed twice, sighed, and let her blonde head sink back on the pillow more than half exhausted.

I reached forward and kissed her softly on those full and accepting lips. Then I put one hand out and turned up the monitor.

". . . then it is agreed." The voice was in German, but not sloppy *Schwyzer*. It was the *Hannoversche hoch-Deutsch* every Swiss knows and few of them use in conversation. We were being nice and formal. "You will follow me up in the car, bringing the two of them with you. My principal will then transfer the money, as arranged, at the chalet in Graubünden."

"All right. That ought to be satisfactory." This was Legras's voice; I'd know it anywhere. "Now if there are no other objections. . . ."

I heard a grunt from Sardou; then, however, a

new voice broke in. "No, no," it said. "It is too dangerous. The transfer can be done on neutral ground. No, I don't like it at all. What if your principal decides to doublecross us?"

There was some discussion of that, the four voices muddling it all up together. I turned to Traudl, who was struggling into her pants now. "Who's that?" I said.

"That's the big boss," she said. "Legras's superior. The one who took over the whole operation when it reached Switzerland. Whether he's the actual man who dreamed up the plot isn't clear. I don't think so. But he's the highest-up of the people I've listened to so far, and the conversations have yet to mention a person higher up in the scheme of things."

I leaned forward, listening. The big cheese? Who could it be? My mind went racing back through the lost list of people I'd been connected with in this affair, searching. I'd heard that voice before, I could swear to it. But who?

SEVENTEEN

"Traudl," I said. "What kind of accent is that guy speaking with? The big cheese, I mean?"

"I don't know," she said. "It sounds like the sort of international accent a person develops when he speaks and understands not only many languages, but many dialects of those languages as well. It could be British. It could perhaps be that of a supremely well-educated and well-traveled American. Why?"

"I have the funny idea that I've heard the voice before—but I haven't heard it speaking German."

"Nick." Her voice was soft and low again, without that touch of pain and desperation again. Only cure for what ails you, I say. Bless her heart, she seemed to agree. "Turn up the monitor, please."

I did. " . . . all right. I'll agree to it then." It was the big shot speaking once more. "But the price goes up."

"Goes up?" the "contact" said. "But we agreed—"

"You know my terms. And I know more than you think I know. I know your principal knows good and well who one of our . . . captives is. And I think he does not want her only for sexual reasons. I think he knows how powerful it will make him if he can hold her over her father's head. If he can use this to force her father to—to political decisions which he would not otherwise be making. If he—"

This touched off another squabble. I turned to Traudl. "Hey," I said. "Who is this mysterious type up on the hill in the chalet above Chur, anyhow?"

"I don't know," she said. "Except that he is very rich and powerful and that he is not Swiss. And," she said with a sigh, "getting through to him will cost us some effort. That 'chalet' they are talking about is in an almost inaccessible place. And we will be doing the climb by moonlight at best, if we are lucky and there are no clouds. And once we get close it will be like a fortress. But listen. They're talking again."

Indeed they were. ". . . what of the other one? The little American? Angelina Negri?"

"All right. All right." It was the "big cheese" talking. "The price goes up. But I toss her into the bargain. For the private pleasure of your—ah—principal."

"The hell you will!" came a familiar voice. Angie! "You can't do this to me, you son of a bitch. You can't sell a woman to some freaked-out greaseball like that as if she were some sort of piece of furniture—"

"Silence," said the big shot. "You have no say in the matter. For all practical purposes you *are* a piece of furniture. Besides, I'm not selling you to him. I'm giving you to him. And you must remember, you lost all proprietary rights to yourself when you opposed us."

"Now, damn you—" She started to say something else, but her words were cut off short. Somebody clapped a hand over her mouth, then—if I was any judge of such sounds—replaced it with a gag. I could hear her muffled screams.

"Poor Angie," Traudl said.

"Well, honey, we'll get her the hell out of there. And somebody is going to pay through the snout for all this. For Matt and Angie and everybody."

"Listen," she said. "It sounds as though they're winding up."

". . . you go ahead with the two girls. I will take the Negri woman in the car with me. We will both follow *you,* my friend. And God help you if there are any slip-ups—or any doublecrosses."

"I assure you. . . ."

"That's all right. Just remember what I said. Now: let's go. The quicker the better."

The voices faded as the speakers left the room. They were talking inconsequentially about overcoats and car keys. I switched off the monitor. "Okay," I said, "let's skedaddle down that goddam hill to the car."

Hidden in the grove we watched the two cars head out toward Highway 3. I was just putting the Mercedes in gear when Traudl touched my arm.

"Here," she said. "If we stay closely behind them on the fast highway they will surely spot us. I have already got a description from the tapped phone line of where the chalet is, and Matt has already driven there once and—how you will say it? 'Cased the joint?' "

"That's how Matt would have put it, all right. But if we don't take the highway how the hell do we get there?"

"There is still the old road. It is steep, and it is a good deal slower. But it gets there, all right, and we will not risk having them see us on the way. It would be a terrible thing to get this close and then spoil everything by—what is the phrase? Tipping our hand?"

"That's the phrase." I shoved the car in first and eased out into the road. "Lead on."

She wasn't kidding about the road being slower and curvier. The new one curved gracefully below us, in wide sweeping strokes; we followed the natural curves of the hills above the Walensee, climbing slowly to the wooded terraces of the Kerenzerberg. After a time the road became harder and harder to see below us. Instead we got gorgeous panoramas of the Churfirsten—giant rock outcroppings, barring the Valley of the Upper Rhine from the low alluvial plains the Linth River flowed into from the Glarus Valley to the south.

For a long time she didn't talk. Then she nudged my arm. "Nick," she said.

"Yes?" I kept both hands on the wheel, swinging it back and forth and braking as the highway dipped and whirled.

"I just wanted to say . . . thanks."

"My pleasure, lady," I said. "Might as well thank me for breathing. You're a terrific girl."

"I *am* thanking you for breathing. I'm thanking you for being there when I needed you. I mean, whether you knew anything about me or not. There are times when . . . well, when a woman just needs . . . I mean. . . ."

"Well, if you want to call it having a nice male shoulder to cry on, what the hell," I said. I snuck a quick glance at her, sitting there with her fair hair blowing in the wind, and warmed at her quick smile. "Look, men need that kind of sudden impulsive warmth now and then too. Don't let the propaganda fool you. We're vulnerable just the same way you are."

"I understand. I . . . well, Matt was that way too. He liked to talk tough, and act coarse. It was a way he had, a kind of insulation. And I suppose it was also a kind of poker face, as he said. It put people off their guard if they thought him dull or insensitive or unfeeling. But a woman comes to learn better about a man."

"Yeah," I said. "No man ever knows another man as well as his woman does."

"Matt said you were out of the ordinary. He said that the very fact that you were sensitive was one of the things that made you a superior operative—perhaps, he said, the best of them all."

"The only thing required is that your instincts be good ones," I said.

"And I think your instincts are good ones." She snuggled against me. I could, however, suddenly feel her shudder through the arm she was holding lightly. "God," she said. "Listen to me, making up to you when my lover is no more than hours dead."

"Matt would want you to seek comfort where you can find it. He wasn't the type to demand that you wear sackcloth, or jump on the pyre next to him."

Then my arm tightened up, and she could feel it, and she sat up straight, as straight as I was. Both of us could suddenly feel the tension in our two bodies as we scanned the road ahead. I didn't even have to point. She knew just what I was looking at. And she was taking it in just the way I was doing.

There was a black car up ahead—a fairly recent BMW or something like that. It was going rather slower than we had been going on that twisty road, and now as the driver spotted us coming up behind him he took some pains to make sure we did not pass him. There wasn't much else to do if we wanted to avoid him; the road was a two-laner and there weren't any shoulders on it for turning around.

And he was slowing, slowing . . . and straddling the white line in the middle of the road, making it impossible to pass.

"Son of a bitch," I said. "Is that who I think it is?" But the moment I said it I already knew.

It was the second car—the one carrying the "big cheese" of the kidnap gang and his precious cargo —Angie Negri, his unwilling little present to the mysterious dealer in woman-flesh whom we were seeking.

He slowed. And slowed again. And finally stopped in the exact center of the narrow road.

And just sat there, as if waiting—waiting for something to happen.

"Nick," she said.

I decided to try brazening it out. I honked my horn. I honked it again.

Nothing happened. I reached inside my jacket and loosened old Wilhelmina in her holster.

"No," she said. "If. . . ." She didn't finish the sentence. We looked each other in the eye . . . and I marveled once again at the essential sweetness of her face, with its hurt eyes and soft lips. "Nick," she said. "You are going to . . . just walk up there? Yes, I can tell. Look, I will cover you."

"It's all right," I said. "Maybe something's wrong with his car. And you remember . . . this is the only one of 'em that doesn't know me."

"As far as you know, he doesn't."

"Honey, everything's a gamble. Everything. And as you say, you'll have me covered."

"Yes. Yes." She reached up under her sweater and yanked out a small but deadly-looking Spanish automatic. "At this range I am a dead shot with this. Nick—"

"Yes, Traudl?"

"Here." And she reached up and kissed me. Hard. And it ran chills up and down my spine, the way no woman's kiss had done it for me for a long time.

I got out, the taste of her still on my lips. I slipped Wilhelmina into my left hand, the one away from the car up ahead. I kept my body in the way so they couldn't see it. And just once I looked back at my car. She was crouched in the shady side of the Mercedes's fender, that mean-looking little gun in her hand. There was a look of something new on her face. I couldn't identify it.

Up ahead the front door opened, the driver's door.

A stocky man, holding on to the door, started to get out.

He had silver-grey hair, dressed slightly long in the present-day European fashion. His shoulders were burly and powerful. His hands were empty. No gun.

He turned slowly to meet me. And I'd never seen that well-cut Continental suit before, or the hairdo, or the silvery-grey beard and mustache that effectively hid his whole lower face from me. But I'd seen those eyebrows before, and the eyes beneath them. Gimlet eyes. Eyes that could burn a hole through solid rock. The eyes of the most dangerous man I'd ever met in my whole life.

"Well," he said. "Don't just stand there—"

"I'll be God-damned," I said. "Hawk. David Hawk."

EIGHTEEN

He almost smiled—and reached for a cigar to hide the fact. "Hello, Carter," he said. "I knew you'd be along in a bit." The voice was as gruff as ever, but I knew he was glad to see me.

I suppose I must still have been standing there with my mouth wide open. Now I blinked and said, "Where did you come from anyhow?"

"I might ask you the same," he said. "Angie tells me you came on the case a day after I did."

"Angie!" I said. "You've got her with you?" And then of course I remembered, and went to the window. She already had it rolled down and when I bent over she stuck her head out and kissed me. "Hey, come on out," I said. "I want you to meet somebody."

"No, wait," Hawk said. "Let's get these damned cars out of the road. Then we can talk strategy. There's a little *gasthof* up the road, and the *Herr Ober* is an old French Resistance buddy of mine. Get in the car and follow me."

* * *

We hashed it all out over a round of Pilsener. It was like Old Home Week, and the only note of discord was the slightly jealous glances Angie and Traudl kept giving each other from time to time. Nothing serious; they were pros, after all.

Hawk, it turned out, was in this one on his own —"as a favor for a friend," he said. There was more than one Jake Quitman in the world, and one of these had told David about the ring that had kidnapped his daughter into a brothel in Maracaibo, where she died with the D.T.'s four years later. He'd put his checkbook at Hawk's disposal with the notion of smashing the ring completely and making sure every member who didn't wind up pushing up daisies ended up doing time in some really bastardly Tijuana-style slammer.

And here Hawk had wound up right in the middle of my own case, just as it was breaking. Well, that was Hawk. There's one thing that separates the damned good op from the super-op, and the only word I can think of for it is instinct. The super-op—and Hawk was unquestionably one of these, even in what amounted to semiretirement—just happens to be there when the goods are changing hands. Something just tells him it's the right place to be just then.

He'd got on their trail quite some time before, and had infiltrated their organization as expertly as ever. At the right point he stepped in, wiped out a cell of the kidnap ring, and replaced their leader, a guy who'd borne some superficial resemblance to him. The change had taken place just as the group's orders had placed his alter ego in the middle of the Mouchamel kidnap. He'd slipped in slick as a whistle—but there hadn't been any chance up to now to separate the two American kids from Sardou and his pals. He'd settled for the next best thing and separated them temporarily from Angie, for the duration of the trip to Chur anyway.

"How did you find out Angie was one of us?" I said.

"Oh, they told him right off," she said. "My cover's blown, Nick. David saw immediately that he had to take charge or I'd wind up on a pigboat heading for a crib in Tanzania. Thank God he did. Now he's going to deliver me to them in an hour or so, all right—but this time it'll be with breakaway handcuffs and all sorts of hardware stowed away in my underwear like that arsenal of yours. I've got a shiv up my sleeve just like you do, and a gas bomb tucked in my skivvies, just like yours, and—"

I caught Traudl's sharp eye on me. "Who is this critter you're delivering the kids to?" I said to Hawk.

"I don't know," Hawk said. "I could make an educated guess that he's either a head of state in some Middle Eastern country that isn't friendly to the Sheikh—or the second banana in the same outfit. Nobody below that level would draw that kind of water with these jerks I'm supposed to be working for. I do know one thing, though: he knows what he's getting."

"I've been wondering." I stuck up four fingers at the *Wirt*, signalling for another round of suds. "Did the kidnappers themselves know what they had at first?"

"No, I don't think they did. It was only after they'd already snatched the kids and got them as far as Monaco that they really began to understand what sort of bonanza they'd stumbled across. Unfortunately, by then they'd found out you were on their trail."

"How the hell did they do that?" I said.

"Somewhere along the line they caught one of the Pivot boys who'd been following you and put him to the torture. He finally blabbed under massive Pentothal injections. There was another one in Monte Carlo itself, and the son of a bitch recognized *me*. I had to scrag him. He was playing the double agent and he knew I wasn't the bird I was claiming to be. He and his friends had me locked up in a room in La Condamine but I got away and bumped him off before he could blab. I dropped him out the window into a bunch of bushes."

"Yeah," I said. "I found him. He was wearing this." I handed him the watch. "I thought he'd done you in and copped it in the process. So now, not only do your pals know who the kids are, and the jerk who's going to try to buy them tonight. But the goddam Pivot crowd does too."

"Damned right," Hawk said. "And can you imagine what'd happen if the girls fell into *their* hands? What with the balance of power being what it is in the Middle East right now?"

Angie let out a stupefied sigh. "My God. Nick, what are we doing sitting here? Let's get—"

"Angie," Hawk said. "You know that fat briefcase I'm carrying in the front seat beside me? Well, it's a direction-finder hooked up to a bug in their car. I've got a beeper tuned to its frequency in this phony hearing aid I'm wearing. I've been following their conversation with one ear all the way through *this* conversation. Nothing's happened. But I do agree we'd better get on the road. Drink up, everybody." He took the cigar out of his mouth, sighed, and tossed it into the trashcan beside him. "Don't worry. The girls are in good hands, more or less, as long as we don't dawdle too much. The chauffeur on their car is a plant of mine. I hired him back in Zurich. He's an old Interpol covert agent who got invalided out of the service when somebody shot him in the lung."

"Might have known you'd think of everything," I said. "Now: what do we do?"

"Too risky using two cars," he said. "I'm going to tell them I had a flat and had to fix it and got delayed that way. Meanwhile I think I'll take you in with me. In the trunk. This car's been doctored and the trunk has a latch that works from the inside. You can get out any time you want."

"What about me?" Traudl said.

"Too risky," Hawk said. "You'll have to—"

I looked at her. Her big soft eyes had just gone ice-cold. "Hawk," I said. "She's in this too. I didn't tell you they got Matt Keller. Back in Zurich. Traudl and he were old friends. She's as involved in this thing as I am."

Hawk frowned. "Keller? One of the best. I'm sorry to hear that. I really am." He looked at me hard. "Who got him? Not one of these birds I'm shepherding around?"

"I don't think so. More likely Pivot people."

"Okay," he said. "You're on, lady. You join Carter in the trunk."

Angie got up and shot me no more than a moderately snotty glance. "Now to struggle back into my irons."

"Hey," I said. "Take care. I know you can take care of yourself, but. . . ."

"Mmmm," she said, and stepped forward to give me a hug. "You do care. I'll be okay, Nick. David's here to protect me." She grinned up at me. "Incidentally, you did a nice job on Legras before they slugged you. That arm of his . . . you got a nerve. His hand's paralyzed."

"Good. I wish it'd been his family jewels."

"Time enough for that," she said. "Now let's go get 'em."

Before he slammed the trunk lid on us Hawk looked down at us. "Look," he said. "When I get out I'll slam the door on my side hard. If the coast is clear I'll slam it again, immediately afterward, as if I hadn't got it right the first time. If I do that it means wait two minutes and then get out. If I don't, if I slam it only once, you've got a longer wait. Keep a sharp ear out. Okay?"

"Sure," I said. "Don't let anybody rear-end you."

"I won't. And remember if you're stymied there you can get out through the back seat. Just lift that panel at the far end of the trunk."

"Okay." And the lid lowered on the two of us.

"Hmmm," she said. "This is cozy in here."

"Oh, is it, now?"

"Yes. Just move, now, a little that way."

"Hey, that feels good."

"I intended it to. Now, if you'll just. . . ."

"Mmmmmmmm."

"Now put your right hand here, and your left one there. . . ."

"Oh, yeah. Yeahhhhh."

"Well, Nick, I don't believe in being bored."

"Mmmmmm. Me either. But just think of all the lovely scenery we're missing."

"It's almost dark anyhow. Besides . . . mmm, Nicky, do that again, will you please?"

"Dee-lighted. . . ."

"Oh, Nick, that's marvelous. You have such a large. . . ."

"The better to . . . How's this?"

"Even better. Oh, yes. *Yesss. . . .*"

"And this. . . ."

"Oh, God. Oh, God, Nick." And then: *"Ohhhhhhhhh!!!"*

Well, I didn't believe in being bored either.

Meanwhile, the miles clicked away beneath us. . . .

. . . and eventually we stopped. Once with the motor running; that must have been to open a gate somewhere. Then we started up again and drove quite a while. Big grounds, then. Five or six minutes of driving in a straight line, another five of gentle curves as the road rose. Then another halt.

And in a moment the door slammed on Hawk's side.

And slammed again.

"Two minutes," I whispered. And watched the phosphorescent dial on my watch as the second hand swept around. "Are you ready?"

"Mmmm," she said. "Well, I'll get ready if you say to."

"I say to," I said. One minute forty . . . forty-five . . . fifty. . . .

"All right." I pushed the lever and raised the trunk, slowly. . . .

. . . and there he was: the guard they'd put on the area around the cars, right after David had left. His back was to us. I raised the trunk lid, slowly, slowly, hoping somebody'd oiled those hinges.

I stepped down to the ground on my slipover sneaker soles. I slid Wilhelmina out of her holster. I stepped forward.

At the last second he must have heard something. He turned. He managed to say "*Wer ist. . . ?*" And then Wilhelmina's heavy butt caught him on the side of the head. He dropped the big Webley he was holding and his eyes glazed over as he fell. I started looking around for something to truss him up with.

"Here," a voice said beside me, and there was Traudl, a length of slender nylon climber's cord in her hand. "Let me do that. I am good at knots."

"Be my guest, baby," I said. And, watching her deft movements, I was glad I'd done it. Her hands looked like Doug Henning's, in the middle of one of those magic stunts of his.

NINETEEN

The house looked more like a hotel. I wasn't quite sure where we were. It seemed likely we were up one of the tributary valleys that led down to the Rhine, somewhere around Davos. It was quite dark by now, except for the little pool of light we'd been standing in; the moon picked out the shapes of tall mountains rising on all sides of us, and there was an Alpine nip in the chill air, thin and smog-free.

Traudl joined me in the shadows, looking around.

"Not many lights on where you can see them," I said and looked up again at the big structure. "Unless of course the action's all on the other side of the house."

"That may be," she said. She pulled that little Spanish pistol again and checked it out. Her movements were quick, professional-looking. "Nick: wait here a moment. I will check the doors on this side. No, come to think of it, you take the other wing. I'll meet you back here in a moment."

"Okay," I said. "But go easy on the gun. If you can avoid using it, do so."

"I had an idea or two about that." She stowed the gun and pulled out an interesting-looking little implement. It had a knob on either end, like some sort of ladies' dumbbell. Some sort of cosh? Perhaps. But as I looked she moved her thumb—almost too quickly to notice it—and out of one of those knobs shot a six-inch shiv blade, and it didn't make even a whisper coming out. I let one eyebrow go up, and grinned at her.

She did something and the blade disappeared again. "Matt invented it for me. For himself, he preferred a pocket arsenal rather like yours. He knew, though, that a woman can't carry that sort of thing without it showing. This fits in a purse—and I can use it fairly well by now."

"I'll bet you can." I reached over impulsively and hugged her. "Take care. I'll see you back here in a moment."

"Yes." She slipped off into the dark, leaving me thinking about her as I wheeled and moved over to the righthand wing of the big house.

As I rounded a corner I ran right into one of them. This one, however, wasn't wearing livery; he was dressed a lot like I was. He looked at me . . . and then attacked.

He was almost too fast for me. His fist came forward in a powerful karate punch; I ducked, but not completely in time. The blow rattled my brains; I reeled—but instinct took over almost immediately, and the body did things that the brain wasn't able to do. My right foot lashed out, much too quick for my conscious mind to give it orders to that effect.

It caught him in the pills and doubled him over. I bulled forward and caught him in the face, all bent over like that, with a knee. I could feel his nose cave in. He let out a small subdued yelp of pain.

And then Hugo was in my hand, and as he straightened up I slipped seven inches of razor-sharp blade into his innards, right below the place where the ribs came together. I shoved up, hard. This time he didn't make a sound. He just sort of leaned forward until he fell on his kisser.

I bent over his black-clad body, and peeled off his right glove, as black as his sweater. By the dim light of the moon I could see it: the little lever and fulcrum, prominent, in blue.

I looked up at the imposing verandah above me. It wouldn't make a damn bit of sense to come right up the staircase. If someone were up there I'd be a clay pigeon for him. I shook my head and went around to the side. The wall was fieldstone, with nice big chinks for fingers and toes; I went up it as easily as if it'd been a ladder.

I took a deep breath before poking my head over the top, cautiously. There was a guard there. But I didn't see how I could get at him without having him see me. He stood out in the open, armed with a mean-looking Schmeisser machine pistol. This one wore livery, just as the car guard had. And his eyes swept the porch . . . I ducked just in time.

I went back down the wall more cautiously than I'd come up. And went around the back of the house. The moon went behind a cloud and when it reappeared I found myself standing on the edge of a sheer drop, one so precipitous that when I leaned over, a moment later, I couldn't see bottom at all.

The house just went straight up, four floors or

more, and there was a sort of observation deck at the top with a lookout tower. There were lights on up there, at the top, and the observation deck was brightly lit, as if somebody were throwing a party. I could even hear the murmur of voices. I looked down again; the whole big stone house, with its two side wings, was perched precariously on a cliff over a dizzying abyss. And as the moon came completely out from behind the clouds, I could see that that view from the observation deck must really be a honey in the daytime. I still hadn't any idea which valley we were in, so I couldn't identify the peaks nearby, but the panorama couldn't have been more spectacular if the scene had been art-directed by Gustave Doré and then painted on the world's biggest backdrop.

If Traudl didn't find a chink in their armor over in that other wing—and I had a strong hunch she wouldn't—I might well wind up having to scale that goddam wall. Right over that yawning drop. In the dark.

"Nick," Traudl said in that soft voice of hers. "I ran into one of them. I had to . . . finish him."

"Me too," I said. "How was he dressed?"

"The same sort of livery the guard at the parking area was wearing. Why?"

"Oh, nothing," I said. But I filed the information away. "Is there a way in from that side?"

"No. Not without attracting too much attention. There is a guard at the front door . . . and another at the side door. Both of them are excellently placed."

"Well," I said, "there's no other choice. I've got to go up the wall. On the other side."

"*Nick.* I saw the other side. It's impossible."

"Not if you have some more of that climber's rope with you."

"I have plenty. But Nick—"

"Oh, I've done worse climbs, in worse circumstances. That isn't the same as saying I liked any of 'em. I don't like this one. But. . . ."

"Nick. I must come with you. I am a good climber. I was the second woman to climb the *Weissturm.* The north face, mind you."

Let me tell you, *that* got my attention. The *Weissturm* was a mountain that didn't *have* an easy way up. A mountain that had killed over two hundred climbers to date, it was fourteen thousand feet high, and with winds that could blow a lichen off the rock. "If you're kidding me along. . . ."

"Okay," I said, "You've convinced me. But—"

"There will be no buts," she said. "Nick, darling, we will conquer this thing as if it were Annapurna."

"You're on," I said.

The valley at the back of the chateau was a smaller version of Yosemite: a hanging valley, one whose guts had been gouged out by a glacier sometime during the Ice Ages of the Pleistocene. I was sure there'd be a whole raft of little rivers stranded up on the tableland above, and that, in the wet season, they'd all have spectacular little waterfalls flowing right over the lip of the valley and falling hundreds of feet to the rocks below before trickling their way down to the main tributary and roaring all the way down to the Rhine near Chur. The same water that dribbled its way over these cliffs would wind up going over the falls at Schaffhausen, and from there through the wine country in Germany and the deep gorges farther north all the way to the North Sea, six hundred miles away.

It'd be a lovely sight in the daytime from up here.

I was glad I couldn't see more of it right now.

She went first. "What?" she'd said. "Let you go on top of me? And *me* have to catch *you* if you slip? A hundred and eighty pounds of you?"

And now, one storey up, I could look up and see her lithe little body at work, her tight little dancer's-style butt sticking out above me. She'd kicked off her sneakers and tackled the chinks and niches barefoot, and now all that showed of her, when the moon went temporarily behind a cloud, was her white hands, sticking out of the sleeves of that black sweater, and the white soles of her little feet.

Now, as the moon came out again, I could also spot the length of light-colored rope she had coiled around one shoulder. She'd pulled it out of her pocket and looped it around her free arm just after passing the first floor.

I was hugging the wall, taking my time. The route she'd chosen up the wall was a good one, all in all—it gave us some natural aid, passing as it did two waterspouts and a flagpole—but it had its disadvantages. One of these was the matter of passing closely by an open window. She was edging closer to it now.

And all of a sudden the light went on in the window, and hands inside the room reached down and shoved the window up!

She froze to the wall. The light inside left her highly visible up there clinging to the stones outside.

And just then a head stuck itself out. And the guy inside the window looked at her, and saw her.

I slipped Wilhelmina out of her shoulder holster.

Hanging on with both feet and one hand, Traudl, thinking fast, swung the first thing that came to hand—the rope—at this face. The coil slipped around his neck.

She dug in and yanked hard, just once.

He teetered . . . and fell forward.

Off balance, top-heavy, he swung over, vaulting over his hands in a beautiful headfirst somersault. He started to holler something . . . but the sheer terror of it, seeing yourself falling headfirst down a mountain, seeing the rocks come rushing up to meet you—it must have taken his breath away.

I looked up at Traudl. Her thumb and forefinger met and made a round O. Digging her bare toes into the chinks, she continued her slow-but-sure way up the sheer wall.

TWENTY

Now, however, a wind was rising, swooping up from that hanging valley below us, bringing a February-like chill with it. My fingers had already begun to ache.

One of the worst things about it was that the winds were blowing away the sounds coming from above, on the observation deck area. I'd wanted to hear a little more of that, and now I couldn't make out a thing. It was all buried in the low *whoooosh* of the wind.

I gritted my teeth and continued the slow upward climb. And as I did I happened to look up to where my hand was reaching for a fingerhold on the rough stones.

First one flake fell on my dark sweater, then another.

Snow! In midsummer! A freak cold snap, with a combination of weather factors that produced not rain but a light powdery greasy snow. The kind that turned to slush the moment it touched something warmer. Like my sweater. Like the sheer rock face we were trying to climb, at night, in a brisk wind, with a thousand-foot drop directly beneath us.

I looked up at Traudl again. Just as I did her foot slipped and her whole body went down with it, to the length of those strong little arms of hers. She dangled precariously, her bare feet swinging, swinging. . . .

I bit down hard and headed up her way, picking the tempo up a bit despite a grim feeling in the pit of my stomach that rushing things right now wasn't the right thing to do. But as I looked up I could see her get one foot in place in a niche and use the other to scrape away the slush in a second cranny before sticking her freezing toes into it. In a moment she had righted herself and was making for the last stretch she had to climb.

I was breathing a sigh of relief and checking my own handholds as I followed her up.

I could see a bit of the stone balcony now. It was made out of the same kind of stuff, and after about the same pattern, as the way the WPA and CCC people used to make Alpine sundecks on Forest Service lodges back during the Depression. The stone floor extended all the way to the edge, overlooking that sheer drop. But in the interest of safety, hand-hewn stones had been piled up at intervals to make support posts for a guide rail rough-cut from huge softwood logs.

There was a chance, a bare chance, that if one of us stuck his kisser up over the edge, below that guiderail, nobody would necessarily notice at first. We could at least look around and see the lie of the land. At least, that was the way I was hoping it would happen.

The damned trouble was, it was all going to be happening in bright light—and we wouldn't know anything at all beforehand. The damned wind whipping the sounds above us away like that kept us from hearing what was going on up there. They could all have ducked back inside, seeking shelter from the wind—and we might have a free shot at climbing over the top and sneaking up on them. Or they could all be standing out there on the deck admiring the view. And armed to the eyes.

Traudl looked down my way just now. I motioned to her to wait for me. I dug in hard and inched my way up to meet her.

When our faces were even she smiled painfully and said, "My God, Nick, my hands and feet are freezing."

"Poor baby," I said. "I'll bet they are. Look, I'm going to climb way over there on the corner. Let me look first. Then I'll duck back down and nod yes or no. Okay?"

"All right," she said. "Then if the coast is clear I'll climb up and over, and you cover me."

"Okay." I patted my chest, where that distinctive Luger handle jutted out. "Wilhelmina here seldom misses anything at short or medium range."

"Make sure she doesn't change her mind. Woman's privilege, you know." She smiled. The smile was warm and trusting. One of her hands snaked out and squeezed my arm. "Now go."

I did. Inching my way along a ledge one toehold at a time, as the wind—it was stronger now—

whipped at my legs and sent cold chills running up and down my spine. The snowflakes were larger now, and were coming thick and fast. In an hour there'd be a sizable pile of it on any flat surface left around. Well, our timing could have been better—we could have picked a warm night—but it could also have been a hell of a lot worse. We could have come up, say forty-five minutes later. And by now we'd have wound up decorating some rocks umpty-ump hundred feet down, both of us.

At the far left corner of the deck I loosened Wilhelmina in her holster and replaced both hands on the rocks. Then I inched up—hell, millimetered up would be a better term for it—and finally stuck my head over the edge.

We were in luck for now. They'd all gone back inside—but there was a big glass wall to the room that faced the deck. Inside, with the glass door shut, you could see a number of people standing and talking, drinks in hand. One of them was David Hawk. One of them was Legras. I caught one more character profiled against a half-drawn drape that, from the size and stance, had to be Sardou. The rest had their backs to me. There was a roaring fire going in a big walk-in fireplace across the room.

I leaned down and signaled to Traudl. And as I poked my head over the top, Wilhelmina now in one hand, I watched her slip over the top and tip-toe on bare feet to the wall, behind one of the drapes, barely out of their line of sight.

As she did I saw Hawk casually look out the window. He followed her dash across the slippery porch with his eyes—but didn't betray her by so much as a blink. Then his eyes scanned the roof and caught mine. Again not a nod. But I knew damned good and well he had us spotted. And I could see him leading the person he was talking to away from the window, toward the bar that was set up beside the big fireplace.

Traudl nodded to me. The automatic was in her hand, and she looked ready for anything. I shoved Wilhelmina back in the holster and climbed up and over.

I'd just got my feet under me and was scrambling to a standing position when one of them, inside, happened to turn my way—and for one terrible moment he looked me right in the eye.

He barked an order to somebody inside . . . and instead of my seeing one of them come charging out that glass door, I watched as a door opened in the stone wall behind Traudl's head and a guy wearing that house livery of theirs moved out behind her, jamming another of those Schmeissers into her back.

"You," he said in German. "Throw the gun over here . . . or I'll cut her in half." His voice was harsh and raspy, his eyes small and gimlety. He'd have done it, too. I shoved Wilhelmina out to him just as he was disarming her.

They were standing behind the glass now watching it all. I looked them in the eye one at a time, giving nobody more attention this way than any other, but when I looked into Hawk's eyes for a moment I saw him wink and purse his lips. The message was clear. *Go along with them.*

The man with the Schmeisser prodded Traudl. She went inside ahead of him—and strong hands grabbed her from both sides, yanking her off to someplace I couldn't see. The man with the gun stooped to pick up my Luger and turned back to me. "Now you," he said.

I preceded him inside. When he slammed the door shut I let out an involuntary shiver. Until I got inside the warm room I hadn't really had time to be conscious of just how damned cold it'd been out there.

And I looked around. Just in time. As I did Sardou grabbed my arms from behind. I swung around and recognized his face. And as I swung my head around to the front again Legras stepped forward, one hand—the paralyzed one, I guessed—stuck inside his coat pocket. The other hand was balled in a fist, and he dug nice and low and caught me one in the groin that doubled me over.

For a moment I saw red and yellow spots. Damn, that Legras could hit with that good hand! I saw the next one coming but couldn't do much about it. It caught me in the eye and rocked my head back hard. Dazed, I shook my head and tried to stand erect . . . but the pain in my crotch was too much.

Legras caught me by the hair and forced my head up. *"Vache!"* he said. And the hand let go and backhanded me across the kisser again. He was drawing back to slug me one in the nose when a new voice broke in.

"Here," it said. "No more of that, now. . . ."

I looked up with my one good eye. The other was full of blood now.

The man standing in the door was a familiar face all right. I'd even met him once, some years ago.

"Yehoshua ben Yehuda," I said.

"Yes," he said. "And you are Nick Carter. I don't know the lady. No matter. She doesn't need a name. Where she is going—she and the other one our friend Herr Morgenroth"—he nodded at David Hawk—"brought to us—where they are going they will not need names. They will just be numbers on a door in a waterfront brothel in a swinish seaport somewhere."

"It's your choice," Hawk said, nonchalantly lighting a cigar. "I just sell them. What you want to do with them is your own business."

I looked at the man standing before him. He was looking Traudl up and down, an appreciative expression on his face. "Well," he said. "We have concluded our deal, and have acquired two—no, three—additional items in the transaction. Do you wish to put a price on the extras?"

"No," Hawk said. "The man—do with him what you will. I will throw the woman in. Yes, and the one in the other room too. The deal we made was for the two children. I consider my organization adequately compensated for these. The others . . . gratuitous."

"Good," he said.

I watched his lean face as he eyed Traudl's body.

I knew him pretty well by now. But I'd learned one thing new about him just now. He wasn't onto Hawk. And a damned good thing too. He was one of the most dangerous men I'd ever run up against.

Yehoshua ben Yehuda had been one of the toughest, most dedicated agents of the Stern Gang back in the early days of the Israeli fight for independence. Maybe a little too tough. There were a number of Lt. Calley-type occasions when his night-raid squad hadn't spared the women and children in the course of their harassment attacks both on the British and on the Arab Palestinians.

On Israeli independence, ben Yehuda had quickly found out there'd be no place in the new government for him. He'd founded an extreme right-wing splinter party that had never managed to get many seats in the Knesset, but that had managed to hang on over the years. Rumor had it that he was financed by Zionist ultra-right elements back in the United States—plus by other enemies of the moderate governments in Israel.

When the Likud party had placed the closest thing Israel had ever had to a real right-wing leader in office, some of ben Yehuda's friends had expected the embargo on his participation in Cabinet-level affairs to end. But precisely the contrary had happened. The leadership had known him entirely too well—and had known of his implacable fanaticism, and how dangerous a friend he'd be to a party dedicated to achieving some sort of settlement with the Egyptians.

This had been the last straw for ben Yehuda. He'd stormed out of the Knesset, resigned his seat, and gone directly into unilateral terrorist work, operating outside of Israel and still financed by—well, some said more than American Zionists were among his backers. After all, who would profit most if a strong government like Begin's were to fall, to be replaced by a more conciliatory outfit? The rumors had it he was actually accepting oil money of various kinds and from various sources, for all that his efforts were directed at the wholesale murder of Palestinians.

And now? Now he had purchased the virgin daughter (at least I hoped she were still a virgin) of Sheikh Achmed, and was theoretically in a position to dictate oil terms for the whole Middle East, and ultimately for most of the rest of the oil-consuming world—an area which comprises everything north of Tierra del Fuego. I shuddered inside.

"Here," ben Yehuda was saying. "Gentleman, we have successfully concluded a mutually agreeable deal. I think it is time for something more festive. Something more in the way of entertainment, perhaps. The young woman in the next room—I understand several of you gentlemen have already sampled what she has to offer. But this new one—does she not capture your interest?"

There was a general murmur of approval.

"Very well then," he said. "I have a friend downstairs who will be joining us in a moment, a friend who will doubtless enjoy sharing the entertainment. Meanwhile, let us have a closer look at what we've got."

Traudl struggled in the arms of the big ox who was holding her. "No," she said. "You wouldn't. . . ."

"Wouldn't we?" Ben Yehuda smiled; I could see the gleam of a gold tooth. "Mr. Sardou? Would you like to do the honors? Let's see what she looks like, now. . . ."

Sardou smiled. I gritted my teeth. I was going to kill him for that smile.

He stepped forward and grabbed her sweater by the neck—and ripped it all the way down. She wasn't wearing a bra, and her breasts were soft and pink-tipped in the firelight.

Now he moved those vise-like hands to her trousers—and in a moment she stood naked before us, the warm light of the flames playing on her bare body. Her eyes were horrorstruck, vulnerable. She struggled again in the man's arms, but couldn't move him.

Sardou laughed, shortly. For that laugh I was going to kill him slowly.

"Bind her hands," he said. "Behind her back." And his hand swept up and down her body as the guard yanked her hands together and pulled a pair of cuffs out of his pocket. She shrank away from his touch, disgusted.

As the guard worked the cuffs onto her hands Sardou was undressing, quickly, deftly. And I got the picture. Sardou had done this sort of thing before. *Voilà le cirque.* He was going to bang her for us, put on a little show for us, in case any of us was an impotent old fart who couldn't get it up by any means other than indulging in a little sado-masochistic voyeurism beforehand. It was something Sardou was used to, something he enjoyed doing, this business of putting on his little show. And it was always a little better for him if the girl wasn't interested, and had to be—well, persuaded. . . .

I was trying to figure out whether anyone was watching me closely, and gauging just how far I'd have to move my hand if I wanted to slide Hugo's seven-inch blade out of my sleeve—or, perhaps better, yank Pierre, my deadly little gas bomb, out of my jock. Preparations stopped, though, when a door opened behind me, and a voice—a voice I'd heard before—broke in on Sardou's little circus. "Wait," it said. "I don't want to miss any of this."

I knew who the speaker was now.

TWENTY-ONE

All the eyes turned back to that door—Legras's, ben Yehuda's, Sardou's, the guard's. Every pair of eyes in the room but mine and Hawk's. Hawk, unruffled, kept his eyes on Traudl. His gaze wasn't a lecherous one. He was looking her in the eye, and he was frowning—if that's what you call a look that could blister paint. There was compassion there—but a lot more anger.

I turned around slowly and looked at the speaker.

I'd seen it all before—but it still looked good. In its way.

The woman was vaguely Oriental in the wide-set almond eyes and the coal-black hair and the high cheekbones. The nails of her fingers and of her sandal-clad toes were painted silver with a sheen that glowed in the firelight.

The sandals were almost all she was wearing. That, and burnished gold jewelry here and there, and—it was a concession to the cold of the evening

—a transparent silk cloak thrown over her shoulders but leaving all the secrets of that gorgeous, very un-Oriental body bare to our gaze.

I'd seen that body before. Yes, and felt it too, the skin softer than the silk on her shoulders, softer than satin, with muscles of spring steel under the softness and smoothness. I might well be the only male alive who had tasted the delights of that incomparable body and lived to remember it.

I looked her up and down, remembering.

The neck was tall and proud, and the gorgeous head sat atop it with a regal bearing. No surprise. She was descended on one side—on the wrong side of the blanket, of course—from the last Empress of China, who, rumor had it, had kept a lover somewhere in the Forbidden City—an English explorer who had been captured high in the Chinese Himalayas, hunting for pandas.

The shoulders were smooth and strong. The breasts were high, proud, dark-nippled. The belly was flat. The triangle of hair was small, coal-black. The legs were long and slender.

"Lotus Fong," I said.

"Ah," she said. "Mr. Carter. We meet again, and once again you are in my way. Well, it will be the last time, I can tell you that. I owe you something—a debt I intend to repay tonight."

I remembered that "debt" well. How could I have forgotten, with that seven-foot devil Chiang —her eunuch bodyguard, a mute with muscles of steel and an icicle where his conscience ought to be, coming up to stand silently behind her?

We'd met in one of the passes between Red Tibet and Nepal, in one of those icy wind-swept saddles between the mountains where the Yellow Robe Buddhists always maintained monasteries, levying tolls for all passers. Now, with the Dalai Lama gone and Buddhism all but crushed out by Tibet's Red Chinese slavemasters, the monasteries were outposts of Chinese border guards—and there I was, trying to smuggle the four-year-old reincarnation of Panchin Lama out of the country where he'd been born and hidden all his young life.

I'd heard of her before. Jesters called her the Dragon Lady's mean stepsister, and they weren't far wrong. Even in the monastery, with Red soldiers about, she went as close to nude as she could stand—and anything she put on that gorgeous body was sure to be chosen not to hide anything, anything at all.

She had it. She flaunted it. And God help the man who lusted after it. Because the worst thing that could happen to him would be to get his wish, once he'd looked on that golden body with the unavoidable yearning in his eye.

Every half moon, as regular as clockwork, she'd take a man. Sometimes she'd choose at random. Sometimes she'd pick someone her fancy had lit upon.

Whichever it was, it didn't matter if he was a neuter or a fairy or whatever. She'd spend a night with him—just one—and she'd find the button that turned him on. And he'd have one glorious night of everything that great beauty and flawless technical proficiency at the arts of love could provide: a night the mere imagining of which would stretch the imagination of the most jaded roué in the world.

And at dawn, sated, exhausted, his body atingle

—he'd be given to Chiang.

And his death would take hours. Some said days.

Chiang was the master of ten thousand deaths, Chinese spies who'd seen her (and escaped; none resisted her. Nobody *could* resist her) said. As his mistress was the mistress of ten thousand joys, Chiang had a horror to follow every joy—and they all ended, eventually, in death. Slow death, death that came a thousand times, one to eradicate each joy you'd tasted.

Chiang, of course, was in love with her. And, having been trimmed of all his external sexual equipment as a boy, he was severely limited as to how he could show it. Virtually the only way, aside from the business of protecting her, was to make sure that everyone who enjoyed her in the ways he could not, lived to regret it.

But not for very long.

I'd been captured and brought before her, and it had been the half moon, and she'd chosen me. And when she'd taken me, in chains, to that tower of hers, with the view of Everest and Mt. Godwin-Austen, I'd looked forward to the experience.

Well, it'd been an experience all right.

She was used to running the show, it seemed. Well, so much for that. It wasn't my style. The moment she unlocked those chains I'd gone after her, and the first notion in my mind had been cold-cocking her with one fist and taking off out that inviting window outside, heading for Nepal as soon as I could find the kid I'd brought with me. But first I wanted a taste of that golden body. And just then the rest of my party had stormed the monastery, and I'd wound up having to knock her cold anyhow. One of my friends had been thrown to his death from a window by Chiang before his partner had turned his M-16 on that seven-foot devil and nearly blown him in two.

Well, he was alive and kicking now. And he looked just as mean as ever. And Lotus Fong? I'd heard the rumors about how her Chinese masters had called her decadent and thrown her out. But I'd never connected her with the international white-slave ring I'd come all this way to bust up. And here she was, big as life, still flaunting it, still daring men to want her, to pay the price.

"Well," I said. "I see you've graduated from whore to procuress. It just goes to show what you can do if you're ambitious."

Chiang stepped forward, and I was getting braced to take him—when the big guard's arms went around mine and pinned them in a grip of steel. I struggled, trying to stomp on his instep—but Chiang was too fast for me. He swung a hand the size of third base at me, and knocked me silly. I almost fell, then caught myself; when I did I instinctively lashed out with one foot, karate-style. Only there weren't any balls there to kick him in. He winced; but his eyes filled with hate, not pain. He clenched one of those leg-of-lamb-sized hands and drew back again.

"Chiang!" she said. "Not now." He pulled back, a glint in that flat eye of his. She turned to ben Yehuda. "How pleased I am that you are satisfied with your purchase. The children—they are where?"

"Down the hall," he said. "They are under guard. I consider the affair a bargain at any price.

The whole balance of power in the Middle East now lies in my hands."

"Then I'm glad," she said, looking him up and down with frankly sexual curiosity in her eyes. That's all it was, though. Eat your heart out, Yehoshua, it's three days after full of the moon and you're going to be a long time hungry if you let yourself get interested in her. And after that you're going to be a long time dead. "Now," she said, leaning against the bar and looking at the two naked people on the thick rug at the end of the room. "Do go on with your little diversion." Leaning back like that, she looked twice as naked as Traudl, who didn't have a stitch on. Maybe it was the jewelry. As I'd learned before, none of it came off, ever —the necklace, the stomacher, the bracelets, the anklets, the rings on fingers and toes. She had a thing about gold, and even the sandals on her feet were held on by little golden chains that ran between those slender toes.

"Splendid," ben Yehuda said. "Continue, M. Sardou. And you, Herr Morgenroth? Would you like to sit over here. . . . ?"

I froze. So did Hawk. And Traudl, looking at him, understood too. Her eyes were full of a new horror, and there was little to choose between it and the horror she had shown when Sardou first touched her.

I looked over at Lotus Fong. Her eyes opened wide. A smile of understanding came over that evil and intelligent face. She crossed her arms over those magnificent nude breasts, making no attempt to hide them—or anything else.

"Herr Morgenroth?" she said. "Surely you are not speaking of *my* Herr Morgenroth?"

Ben Yehuda stiffened. He looked at Hawk. And his hand dived inside his coat, coming out with a wicked-looking Luger. I recognized it and scowled. It was my own—Wilhelmina. "You!" he said. "Turn around!"

Hawk turned. And looked her right in the face.

"Ah," she said, daring Hawk to look her up and down. Daring him to register the pleasant sexual shock we'd all registered at the first sight of her, nude, bejeweled, wearing only the transparent cloak and those golden shoes. Hawk looked her right in the eye as if he couldn't give a damn if she were wearing Dr. Dentons. "Mr. Ben Yehuda. Introductions are in order. This is, of course, not my assistant, Herr Morgenroth. It is, instead, the very dangerous Mr. David Hawk. Mr. Carter's employer—or is it former employer?"

"Hawk?" Ben Yehuda said. He drew back the knurled butt of my old Luger, and for a moment I thought he was going to hit David in the face. Then he relaxed into an icy calm. "Ah," he said. "My mistake. Thank heaven you corrected it for me. No matter. Neither of them will leave this mountain alive." He motioned Hawk to a chair, keeping the gun pointed at him. "Now," he said. "The rest of our little exhibition, please."

I moved forward a hair. A heavy hand fell on my shoulder. I turned, my hand already going for Hugo's slim shape. It was too late. The guy behind me slugged the hell out of me. I saw it coming, but I couldn't do a damned thing about it.

When I awoke the room was empty and the fire was guttering out. There was a spilled drink on the floor, with a cracked glass beside it.

They were gone!

I scrambled to my feet, ignoring my damn splitting headache. I reached inside my sleeve. Hugo was still there. Other than that—and Pierre, my gas bomb, I was unarmed.

How long had they been gone?

I ran to the door and threw it open.

Down the hall there were voices. I tiptoed nearer, hoping against hope . . . but as I approached the open door I knew my birds had flown. What I was hearing was a pair of guards who'd been left behind. "Here," one of them was saying in German, "it's not so bad. So you lose a job. Jobs are dirt cheap. You can always find another. . . ."

"But . . . I didn't expect. . . ."

Right then one of them chose to stick his head out the door—and looked me right in the eye. "Hey!" he said. "You. . . ."

I karate-chopped him in the neck and, not waiting to watch him crumple, came around the corner at the other one, knife in hand. He ran right onto Hugo, a look of terrified surprise in his eyes. I let him hang there for a moment before withdrawing my hand and my knife. He pitched forward.

I bent over the other one and checked him. He was out cold. I relieved both of them of their pistols and, as a second thought, of their keys. Somewhere on those keychains there had to be some car keys. Just in case they'd all left the house already, and there happened to be a spare set of wheels down there in the courtyard.

Then I bounded down that first flight of stairs. As I did another guard, at the foot of the next flight down, stepped out into my way and leveled a machine pistol at me. I didn't wait around to offer him a nice safe target; I threw down on him with one of the big 9mm revolvers in my hands and fired. A bright blossom bloomed on his forehead. His body just sort of crumpled, one joint at a time.

I didn't wait. I bounded right over him, heading for the next landing.

At the second-storey landing there was a big picture window, though, and as I neared it I saw all the lights in the parking lot suddenly blink on, with a terrific glare. It lit up the courtyard below like midday.

And now I heard it—the dull roar of a helicopter coming in for a landing.

TWENTY-TWO

Somebody down below was hollering. I stuck my head to the window and looked around. And as I did four landing lights went on at the four corners of the courtyard, and now there was a brilliantly lit square there for the guy in the whirlybird to land in, with colored lights marking the perimeters. Obviously there wasn't anything special about the idea of a 'copter landing there. Somebody had done this before.

I stood watching there, trying to figure out what the hell I could do to stop it. Now I could see the knot of them, ben Yehuda and his men, getting ready to board. And there—the two little figures in the jumpsuits—that must be the two kids.

The blades of the copter kicked up dust in the courtyard. They all stepped comfortably outside the square. I could see Lotus Fong now, standing statuesque and beautiful in—for a change—a dark cloak, her sandaled feet sticking out below the hem.

And now I looked around at all of them. Ben Yehuda. The kids. Sardou, in a business suit once again. Traudl, in her black outfit, her feet still bare. Legras. The guard who'd slugged me. Chiang, towering over all of them in his outsized Mao suit. Hawk, his hands manacled before him like Traudl's, his face an impassive mask.

The copter came down—then a gust of wind hit it and threatened to ram it into the verandah. The pilot backed off and took it up another thirty feet or so until the wind let up. Then he started settling down again.

There was somebody missing down there. Who the hell was it?

"Haende hoch!" a voice bellowed at me from the landing below. I wheeled, one of the revolvers in my hand—but he had the drop on me, and the weapon in *his* hand was an M-16.

I sighed—and held my hands high, the guns still in them.

And now a figure slipped out of the shadows behind him, and a pale hand bearing a long, stiletto-like knife sliced into the trigger hand aiming that deadly submachine gun at me. There was a gout of red blood, and a cry of pain from the liveried guard. He dropped the gun and held the mutilated arm. And only then did he begin to react.

It was too late. Angie's hand whipped out and sliced him across the guts, right to left. The blade must have been every bit as sharp as Hugo's; it cut through his uniform shirt and jacket, and through the gap I could see the red splash at the middle of his belly. He put his hands to his slashed-open gut—and Angie's knife sliced through his throat for him.

She let him fall.

I let my hands fall.

"Baby doll," I said, "I sure as hell *am* glad to see you."

"Same here, pal," she said. "Toss me one of those guns, will you? You can have the M-16. I'm no good with one of those things, but I'm a good shot with a pistol."

I did better than that. I bounded down the stairs and put the pistol in her hands—and gave her a quick hug in the process. Then both of us looked down from the window above that landing.

The 'copter was having trouble with the goofy gusts of winds that had given Traudl and me so much trouble earlier. It swayed, looking like a puppet dangling from a chain, and kicked up terrible gusts of dust and dirt. "How did you get loose?" I said.

"Those breakaway cuffs. The guard they put on me got ideas. I busted his neck for him—but not before he'd showed that Chink exhibitionist down there in to see me and let her maul me. I—"

"Oh, ho," I said. "You mean—"

"I mean she's a goddam lez, that's what I mean. She may bang a boy now and then, but it's just for the pleasure of knowing she's put him off guard just before she lets that big gook down there go to work on him. No, she showed a definite interest in yours truly." Her voice was full of disgust.

I resolved to keep my own little history nice and quiet—around Angie, anyhow. "Look, the son of a bitch's getting ready to touch down. Let's go."

But she was already a step ahead of me, heading down the last flight of stairs. And the guard at the front door hardly knew what the hell hit him when she came up behind him and cold-cocked him with the butt of that big gun I'd given her.

She stopped dead at the door just as I was coming up behind her.

I looked out. Ben Yehuda was handing the two kids up into that damn copter and climbing in after them. "Shit," I said. "We're too late."

"Nick," she said, "is there any way to disable one of those things?"

"Not without hurting those kids," I said. Then we looked up into the moonlit night sky, still full of light a couple of days after full of the moon.

There was another 'copter up there. Hovering. Waiting.

Ben Yehuda saw it just then, too—and obviously it wasn't something he'd been expecting. I saw his lips peel back in a snarl and an inaudible curse. He pointed up at the sky, and the guard who'd slugged me pointed his M-16 up at the whirly in the sky.

And then all hell broke loose.

It looked like one of those commando raids you used to see in the old WWII movies. All of them, coming out of the shadows all bent over, weapons in hand, wore dark brown jumpsuits made of some sort of neutral cloth that didn't reflect light.

I saw David Hawk grab Traudl's arm and dive for the bushes, his hands still manacled before him. And not a moment too soon, either. A burst of machine-gun fire from one of the running figures sliced through the night and slammed into the wall right behind where they'd been standing.

Sardou had pulled out a pistol of his own and shot down one of the advancing figures. Then a bullet from another of them tore into his shoulder and spun him around. He was still spinning when one of the brown-clad guys caught up to him and swung the dull-metal machete he was carrying. Sardou met the fate of Charles I of England, whose head was buried in a different place from the rest of him.

Legras, his damaged arm still immobile by his side and its unfeeling hand tucked into his pocket, had his own rod out and was blazing away at them. He got two of them, and ben Yehuda, firing from the 'copter, hit another.

"Hey," I said. "That goddam 'copter's going to be getting away." I didn't wait around for an answer. I dived through that big window we were looking through and headed for the copter. As I did I heard her covering shots behind me, and I saw another one of the guys in brown go down. Another one was grappling with Legras. As he did so Chiang, the Chinese giant, came up behind him with a machete he'd took off somebody and lopped off a brown-garbed arm. I didn't stop to watch the rest. I let out a burst of M-16 fire in their general direction, just to keep somebody off balance, and sprinted toward the 'copter.

I barely caught hold of it, grabbing the landing strut with one hand. As I did somebody grabbed my legs. I looked down and brained him with the M-16. Hanging on as the 'copter rose, I squeezed the trigger and fired wildly into the gang of them, without the smallest hope of hitting anything, until the hammer hit on empty. Then I heaved the gun away and grabbed at the strut with my free hand. The last thing I saw, looking down for one split second before the 'copter whirled up and away, was Lotus Fong, that black cloak thrown back over her shoulders for action, her golden body startlingly naked, her little hands occupied with firing a pair of deadly little automatics into the commando unit, with fearsome accuracy.

I don't know just when they became aware I was there. At first I believe they didn't know. You can't easily tell much about the change in weight on a 'copter. You could in a comparable light plane, just as you can tell in a light plane in the dark whether you're rising or falling. The seat pushes up against your ass when you're rising, it falls out beneath you—giving you, sometimes, as close to a feeling of weightlessness as you can get outside of Earth orbit—when you're falling.

That's not true on a 'copter. The seat pushes up against your behind all the time, and if your altimeter isn't working you can be thinking you're going up, up—and you'll be diving into a hole.

I hoped this guy could see well. The damn moon made everything hunky-dory when it was out—but there were those goddam clouds that had produced the snow before, and the moon kept slipping behind them.

Now the moon was out, and I could see the earth falling away below me. Now I could see the real position of the old ex-hotel, perched on the lip of that dizzying abyss, and could see the whole hanging valley spread out below me and the now white-capped peaks across from me, towering above the hole that glacier had dug in the Swiss earth.

Far below I could see the Valley of the Rhine, and ancient old Chur, where the Romans had passed and built a road over the Alps, with its warm little lights and curls of woodsmoke. I fancied I could see all the way over into Liechtenstein, into Austria beyond it.

And now, looking behind me, I could see something else.

That other 'copter. It had taken off from the house and was following us, swooping up away from that precarious location on the edge of the cliff and coming around below us, out of sight of the pilot of the copter I was riding on.

Now, as we leveled out for a moment—to the extent that a whirly ever levels out—I got one leg up over the landing skid and braced myself in a sitting position. And for the first time I could get some idea where the hell we were heading.

The outlook wasn't encouraging. The goddam 'copter was heading Southwest—up the Valley of the Vorderrhein toward the gigantic massif of the Jungfraujoch. Bad, bad, bad. Particularly if we had somebody chasing us.

I looked back.

And I put two and two together.

Of course. The whole goddam thing had been blown to the Pivot crowd along the way—and they'd planned a raid to kidnap the two kids and use poor Meriem Mouchamel for their own ends. Which, even allowing for the fact of theoretically being on the other side, weren't any better, or for that matter any different, than those of Yehoshua ben Yehuda.

Goddam all adventurers. Particularly in a volatile environment like the Middle East. Last place in the world that you need any wild cards in the deck, any officious assholes sticking their oar in and muddling things up. And here's ben Yehuda screwing things up from the Israeli side and screwing the Israelis as much as anybody, and the Code Name Pivot boys screwing things up every bit as badly for the Arab bloc as for the Israelis they professed to hate.

That was who was following us, and that was who had staged that little raid back there. And that was who had designs on those kids up in the 'copter I was taking this precarious ride on.

I sighed. I should have figured it out. Particularly after I'd run into that advance man of theirs just before I'd scaled the wall. Of course. All they had to do was wait until the transfer had been made. . . .

I looked back at them now. They were gaining on us. Below, the tiny lights of Reichenau, Versam, Ilanz sped by. Up ahead, the peaks of the Buendner Oberland loomed on my right, and in the distance I could make out, high above Andermatt, the imposing bulk of the St. Gothard Massif, with the Three Passes area beyond it.

The noise of the 'copter was deafening, and the wind was whistling past me at a hell of a clip. I didn't hear the first shots at all. All I know of them was when I saw the red flashes from those guns in that other 'copter, a blink or so after something whistled by my ear, close. . . .

Just then, however, the moon went behind a cloud, and I was thanking my lucky stars for it. There sure as hell wasn't any place to hide up here.

And one thing was sure.

They weren't aiming at the 'copter itself. Not with a precious cargo like Meriem Mouchamel aboard, somebody whose young life they could trade for concessions worth a lot more, to people of their particular stamp, than money.

No, they were aiming at me. Nick Carter. The damn fool who had been blundering into their way. And at the present rate, if the moon came back out again and there was anybody back in that 'copter who was any kind of shot at all, they'd get me. I was sitting in the suicide seat, the one where you can't win, the one where they mark you dead the moment you sit in it. I was riding for every kind of fall, and the only arms I had on me were the ones I usually carried—less Wilhelmina, who was, I supposed, still stuffed inside ben Yehuda's jacket, and plus the six-shot revolver I'd been carrying when I jumped aboard.

Six shots. To put an enemy 'copter out of commission, and capture the one I was riding in, and bring a desperate international criminal to justice.

And now the moon came out from behind that cloud, and the 'copter following us was a lot closer, and I saw the red flashes again, and again I felt the deadly bees come buzzing past. And now, if I didn't have enough to contend with, it had begun snowing again—blinding, slippery, powdery snow that got in my eyes, that numbed my freezing fingers, that threatened with every flake to dislodge my grasp on that slender strut, to make me fall from my perch. . . .

TWENTY-THREE

Of course I couldn't hear a thing—not even that freezing wind whizzing past. The roar of the 'copter engine was enough to take care of that all right. It didn't matter. The next time one of those bullets went careening by me I didn't need to hear it—or see it either. It tore into the strut I was hanging onto for dear life and nearly shook my hand loose.

I had to do something, and in a hurry.

I yanked that borrowed revolver out and, taking a firm grip on the upright with the other hand, drew a bead on the other 'copter. It was a lousy target at best, with both him and myself swaying like crazy in the wind—and with my hand shaking from the cold. But what the hell, I'd taken worse long shots before.

He let loose another burst at me, and this time it damn near parted my hair for me.

"All right, pal," I said. "You want to play hardball, we'll play hardball. . . ." I took careful aim and squeezed.

Bingo! A star-shaped pattern sprang out in the

middle of his windshield. It must have shook him up a bit; he wavered and fell both back and down, hanging like Pearl White dangling from a clothesline, swaying. . . . Then he righted himself and came back after us again. And I saw the bullets dig into the main body of the whirly, above my head; he'd lost the range and hadn't got us zeroed in again yet.

As he steadied himself for another shot at me I took aim again. As I did a gust of wind hit me hard, and I came very close to falling—and another volley slammed into that strut I was holding onto. I shuddered and looked up. The strut was hanging on by a piece of metal no more than an inch wide now, and it was all in the world that was keeping me from taking a nice little skydive, sans 'chute, into the gorges of the Medel-Rhein far below.

I took another bead and fired again. This time I could see who I was firing at. With the snow blowing right at him, over my shoulder, the guy on the passenger side had to lean out past the window even to see me, much less to shoot at me. And now he leaned out a little too far, and I caught him right between the eyes. He just seemed to slide out the side window and float down, the machine pistol still in his hand.

That settled one thing for the guy following me. He cut off the inside lights in his 'copter, and now I could only see him when the moon came out again nice and clear. I waited, shivering, freezing . . . and then the moon came out from behind a wispy cloud above and I could see his Plexiglas front, the wipers hard at work trying to clear the snow off it, and I drew another bead. . . .

This time it caught him right in the middle of where the driver's body ought to be. Just where I hit him I'd never know, later on. All I would ever know was what I saw now: the whirlybird suddenly going stone crazy with no guiding hand to keep it on course, slipping away to my right, going into a wild spin as his body hit the joystick and flipped it over, tailing off, falling far behind, falling, falling. . . .

Eventually there was a red burst of flame on the hillside far below.

I shook my head, trying to clear the snow out of my eyes, and stuffed the pistol back inside my sweater.

Three shots left. Three. . . .

The strut shook.

I looked up. The damn thing was hanging by a thread, it seemed like—the snow had picked up, and I couldn't see much now—and if I didn't find something to hold onto damn quick, there might not be anything left to hold onto, now or ever.

The strut shook again—and the inch-wide strip that was holding me up became a half-inch-wide strip.

I got my feet underneath me now and—very carefully, mind you—tried standing up. Holding onto that ruined strut for dear life, and doing as little as possible to rock the boat.

And now, standing, I could reach the first of the handholds somebody'd welded onto the side of the whirly, making a kind of ladder to climb up on. I got one hand on the bottom one and the other hand on the one just above it. My hands were so cold it was all I could do to hold on. . . .

. . . and guess what? That would just manage to be the time when the strut snapped, and fell out from under me, and hung down, its own weight dragging it down and making it flap in the wind. . . .

Now *that's* the sort of thing you notice, piloting a whirly. Since it only happened on one side, it unbalanced the bird itself, and the damned 'copter swayed. If I hadn't had a good two-handed hold on those ladder rungs I'd have been shaken off right there. As it was I managed to haul myself up, hugging the slick snow-covered surface, and get one foot, then two, securely on the bottom rung of the ladder.

And that was when ben Yehuda put two and two together. And decided there might just be some correlation between the fact that that second 'copter had suddenly ceased to be a problem—and the fact that something was wrong with the balance of the one he himself was riding in.

And, leaning out into the snow, he looked back —and down.

And saw me. . . .

The thing that saved me was the fact that he had to reach back inside the cab for his gun.

As he did I grabbed for that borrowed revolver. And hauled myself, one-handed, painfully up the ladder another three rungs. . . .

As I did he leaned back at me again. And shot the pistol right out of my hand.

Good old Wilhelmina. She never missed. Only this time I'd have settled for a little uncharacteristic inaccuracy. It wasn't to be, however. His slug hit my revolver and knocked it out of my cold-numbed hand. It shocked him as much as it did me, considering I was right on top of him when he did it.

There was only one thing to do.

I reached out and grabbed his hand, the one holding my old friend Wilhelmina. I turned the old girl ninety degrees, trapping his forefinger in the trigger guard. He howled silently—the wind sweeping his words away into the darkness below—as I broke his finger for him and took my old gun back.

And then I got him one right in the face. His nose disappeared in a flash of red. And the light in his eyes disappeared. He spun out, top-heavy, and tumbled over backward into the abyss.

I sighed. *One down, one to go . . .*

I hoped to God the pilot was nice and busy now. Too busy to get ideas about using the girls as a body shield if I went in that open side window.

Why not climb over the top and try going in *his* side? So that he wouldn't be able to hide behind the kids? So that I might have the element of surprise riding for me in this business?

I raised my head up over the top of the tail end of the fuselage, blinking against the freezing snow. There was a four-foot gap between the ladder on one side of the 'copter and the one on the other side. If I could get close enough. . . .

I stowed Wilhelmina in my sweater and climbed up to the crossover point. Twice I had to wipe the snow out of my eyes. Once the wind caught me and almost threw me off the whirly into the upper reaches of the Vorderrhein a couple of thousand feet below. I reached out, trying to grab that elusive handhold on the far side of the whirly.

There *are* some things a 'copter pilot can do, however, to get rid of an interloper like me. This guy knew some of them. Suddenly we began swaying wildly. I nearly lost hold. He abruptly dropped us a hundred feet or so. The bird almost fell out from under me.

And then as he leveled out, presumably to set up another attack on my equilibrium, I reached out again for that ladder-rung on the other side.

And got it this time.

My heart in my mouth, I swung one leg over. Then the other. And got both feet on the ladder, one hand holding me close.

He looked out and around.

I shot him between the eyes.

I grabbed his arm and yanked. And now that damned 'copter started fishtailing. Spinning. Started the long, long spin that ends on the hillside below every time, if you let it, ends in a bright burst of red flame, followed by pitch-black petroleum smoke.

I yanked again. His upper torso came out, but damn it, he was locked in by the same sort of seat belt ben Yehuda had disdained.

And then he came loose in one big yank, and fell headfirst out of the spiralling 'copter. And I hauled myself up and in, and got one leg up and over, and got the surprise of my life.

There was little Meriem Mouchamel, sitting pretty as you please at the controls of the 'copter, hands on the stick, busily engaged in a thoroughly professional-looking—and totally successful, as it turned out—attempt to bring the stricken bird under control. Her smile looked a little strained, but it was all gorgeous brown eyes and full red lips for all that.

"Hello," she said as I pulled myself inside and

closed the side door behind me, shivering. "You must be Mr. Carter. I talked to Miss Negri . . . to Angie. She never doubted for a moment that you would save us."

"Save you?" I said, grinning. I nodded a happy hello to redheaded Sandy Fleischer on the other side; she was a lot less intense than her pictures had made her look. "My god, you seem to be doing just fine as it is. Where did you learn to pilot one of these things?"

"I bribed one of my father's pilots," she said. "He was in love with me, I believe. At any rate he was ambitious. I told him if he would teach me I would speak to my father about getting him a job at my family's estates. I did . . . but he did not last long. My father has a terrible temper."

"So I hear," I said. "That's one reason why I've got to get you back to him. Immediately. And have you waiting for him when he arrives in Washington."

"Yes," she said. "All dressed up looking young and virginal in a pinafore or something. I understand. I understand all of it, I believe: the killings, the kidnappings, the deal with this man ben Yehuda. There is only one thing I do not understand."

"What's that?" I said.

"I do not understand where we are going. I have no idea where we are. How then would I have any idea where it is that I am supposed to land." She smiled that gorgeous smile at me again. "Besides, Mr. Carter, I've never landed one of these things, with or without a broken landing gear. Would you perhaps like to take over now?"

* * *

I turned us around and headed back toward Chur, figuring that it'd be easier to find reliable air transportation there. As I approached the area where we'd been I looked down and saw the flames pouring out of the windows of ben Yehuda's old fortress—the one whose sheer walls I'd climbed with Traudl only a couple of hours before—and saw the fire trucks clustered in the courtyard. Everybody'd be gone by now, I figured. I turned and headed down the road to Chur.

For some reason I decided to stick closer to the road. The valley I was in was wide enough to allow it, and I was damned tired by now of the high-up, wide-open spaces. The snow had cleared by now. I found it expedient to follow the sparse traffic down the road toward the seat of Canton Grisons.

"Mr. Carter," Sandy Fleischer said suddenly. "Down below—"

"Yes?" I said, instantly alert. I looked down. Two of the cars up ahead were driving like maniacs, weaving in and out of traffic, going around curves in controlled skids. . . . "Hey," I said, "you don't suppose. . . ?"

"I certainly do," she said. "That front car . . . we were driven up here by that car. Meriem: don't you recognize it?"

"Yes!" Meriem Mouchamel said beside me, grabbing my arm. "Mr. Carter . . . the car Legras and Sardou brought us here in . . . it had a left-hand front headlamp that was seriously out of alignment, the way this one is. I . . . I think Sandy's right. And look—the other car is chasing him. If . . . but no. This has to be the one."

"You could very well be right," I said. "They're sure acting odd, both of them. Yeah, and that one chasing the first one, that could very well be the car David Hawk was driving when I ran into him on the road. It's the same make and color."

"Goodness," Meriem said. "Someone is getting away."

"Yes," Sandy chimed in. "Mr. Carter . . . can't we do anything?"

"I can try," I said. "But first I've got to find out something."

"What's that?" Sandy said.

"Who's who. Even if we know the cars are the right ones, we don't know for sure who's in them. That could be Hawk up front, for instance, escaping from Legras."

"Oh, dear," she said.

"That's okay," I said. "One way to find out. . . ." I swooped down and passed the second car and waggled the 'copter's rear end seductively at it. No response . . . but yes there was. Someone down there honked back.

And somebody in that first car leaned out of a window, looked up, and put a bullet through my windshield, pretty as you please.

I looked around at Meriem now. "You know, ladies," I said, "I'm getting damned tired of getting shot at."

"I understand," she said. "I'm equally tired of being kidnapped. And sold. And. . . ." She pursed her lips angrily.

"Okay," I said.

I didn't smile anymore. Enough of the preliminaries.

Endgame time.

TWENTY-FOUR

There was Chur coming up, though, and those narrow streets with all those belfries sticking up would make a hell of a lousy place for a body to be chasing anybody in a helicopter. I started looking around for a way to head them off—and happened to look at the petrol gauge. "Oops," I said. "Getting low on something for this damn thing to drink."

"Oh, goodness," Meriem said. "Yes you are. Oh, my. We've got to. . . ."

"Meriem," Sandy said. "There is something. They're coming in on the Arosa road—the one we came in through. Do you remember that terrible hairpin turn on the road just as it left Chur and doubled back? Where the road starts climbing again? There was a nice view, I remember—and the car had to come to something like a dead stop coming around that 180-degree turn. . . ."

"Yes! Yes!" Meriem said. "She's right, Mr. Carter. They'll have to virtually stop dead there.

When they do . . . if we could contrive somehow to put an obstacle of some kind in their way. . . ."

I looked down at the two cars, winding their way down the hill, their headlights cutting into the night. "Maybe we can do better than that," I said. I looked down to the place where the lights of the city shone bright and warm. Snow lay on the little medieval town and the moonlight shone on it. And now I could see the overhang, and the hairpin turn, and the cars descending toward it.

"Okay," I said. "Here we go." I banked away from them in a long curve, slowing, descending . . . and below us the cars braked and skidded, taking the turns precariously in the snow. I didn't know for sure who the hell that was driving, but I'd bet it was Hawk in the rear car. He stuck to Legras's tail like somebody being dragged behind on a chain. Well, that was okay. If anyone could hold the road on that kind of a chase, Hawk could. And Angie, inside, she could take it. She wouldn't get the vapors. I grinned as I saw the red burst of fire from the second car. She was shooting at them, and not too inaccurately either. One of her shots struck sparks from that car down there.

"What are you doing, Mr. Carter?" Meriem said. "The road. . . ."

"It's okay, Meriem," Sandy said. "I see what's happening. He's coming down on the road the right way. It's just that this way they can't get in much of a shot at us as we come in. Right, Mr. Carter?"

"Right, Sandy," I said. "And the name is Nick —both of you. Hang on, now." And I brought the 'copter down in a steep descending bank, heading for that wild switchback—I could see it very clearly

now—on the terraced hillside.

The cars below us braked, slid, righted themselves, and accelerated again, heading down that hill toward that rendezvous. And now I could see someone leaning out of that rear window and aiming at us. I tossed Wilhelmina at Sandy. "Hey," I said, "if you can figure out the drill on using this old girl, take a couple of potshots at them. I figure you ought to owe them something yourself. Right?"

"Darn right," the redheaded girl said. And expertly jacked a round into Willie's chamber. "I can usually hit something on the flat. I don't know about on the fly."

"It doesn't matter," I said. "Mainly I want them to stay rattled. If they know somebody's shooting at them from up here they won't make so much of a problem, shooting at me."

"Okay," she said. "Here goes." She got off two quick shots; then Willie's magazine gave out. "Damn."

"It's all right," I said. "Matter of fact, I think you nicked them once. Now hang on. . . ."

That lead car—an old-model Citroën—hit the turn, hit the brakes, skidded, hit the brakes again, fishtailed. . . .

. . . and then we came in in a fierce dive, tailing off at the last moment.

That hanging piece of landing strut that had nearly cost me my life swung around as we pulled away at the last possible split-second—and, whipping back toward them, slammed fiercely into the driver's side, smashing in that whole side of the car.

And somehow the driver—he couldn't have lived through that, not for long anyhow—seemed to

have hit the gas in one last spasmodic motion. Low gear or no, he shot forward—and went over the embankment as pretty as you please.

And in a moment the townspeople of Chur had a nice little problem for the town fire trucks to solve.

We all got back together for a few minutes before Angie was due to ferry the kids posthaste back to New York—twelve hours before deadline. Hawk, as usual, turned out to have some leftover pull with the Swiss government. He squared the whole matter with everybody with two trunk calls to Zurich and Berne.

Meanwhile I was talking to the fire department. I came back to the group of them, sitting around a big 500-year-old oak table in the local *Gasthaus*. They were sitting before a roaring fire, each one of them with a tall glass of suds in hand. "Interesting," I said. "I thought you said Lotus and her boyfriend were in the car."

Hawk looked up, his eye suddenly hard. "They were, Nick. I saw them get in."

"The fire boys say there were only two bodies, and neither of them was a woman. And neither of them," I added, "was a seven-foot Chinaman."

"Damn," said Angie. "Somehow I'd hoped we'd seen the last of Flossie the Flasher. Well, maybe she'll write us when she finds work. In a burlesque house, maybe." She turned up her glass and drank lustily.

"I understand," I said. "I like to close the book on things whenever I can myself, but . . . well, damn it, we don't even know how many of the Pivot crowd we got. Or—more importantly—how

many there are left. All we know is that—very likely, anyhow—we put a crimp in their style for a while."

"No more than that, Nick," Hawk said. "That's a big and well-disciplined organization. I'll let you have a look at the file."

"File?" I said. "I thought the whole AXE file had been destroyed."

"It was convenient to have everybody think so," Hawk said. I was beginning to get the picture; Hawk had masterminded the breakup of AXE—partly to go after the Pivot group; but, more importantly, to go into deeper cover. We had become known too widely, and the political climate worldwide required greater skill and secrecy than ever before.

I excused myself to make a call to Mame.

The house phone, however, was dead. The waiter directed me next door, where a neighbor, he said, would let me use his phone if I put up the cash. I thanked him and went out the door into the cool of the evening. The moon shone brightly on the newly fallen snow, and it was one of those lovely brisk nights when you can see the Milky Way all the way down into a small town like Chur. Most of the cloud cover was gone, drifted down the valley of the Vorderrhein toward the tall peaks and the Valais. I sighed and breathed in the cold, clear air.

And that deep breath was very nearly my last. A hard arm, not much smaller or weaker than King Kong's, clamped around my neck and cut off my wind. I reacted as quickly as I've ever reacted to anything, digging elbows into his ribs hard and stomping down hard on his instep. Both moves should have hurt him; but it was like slugging a

stone statue. No response at all. And I couldn't get any breath. . . .

I started coming out of it—I don't know how much later. I'd lost count of anything. I awoke with my face to a warm floor, and looked up, shaking my head, to see a roaring fire before me, almost the duplicate of the one in the *Gasthaus*. But this one wasn't in any guest room. It was in the big hall of a sizeable chalet-type building, and there was all sorts of heavy oak furniture around.

I sat up, feeling my neck.

Standing before me in a room lit only by the fire was Lotus Wong, and—except for the gold that shone everywhere on that smooth body of hers—she was naked again, the way she liked to be whenever she could manage it. She stood, letting the warmth from the flames play over that long beautiful body of hers, looking down at me. I looked her up and down. She was fantastic; the warm gold of her skin was set off by the cold Arctic glint in her eye and the cold of the metal that glimmered at neck and belly and wrists and ankles.

And now I saw her as she was.

The cool silver of her nails was the cold sheen of an eagle's claws, and the eye was that of a predatory bird. And the smile on her face wasn't a smile at all, it was the anticipatory grimace a carnivorous animal goes into involuntarily just before it's ready to feed on human flesh.

"Well," I said. "I couldn't get you anything, could I? A nice glass of hemlock? A Mother Hubbard?"

"Interesting," she said. "You are trying to con-

vince me that you do not desire me. That you are immune to whatever charms this body of mine may possess. . . ."

"Balls," I said. "I know myself. There might well be some way you could still turn me on. I'm not Superman and I'm not a fag. And you know quite a bit about men. Enough to play with them, and manipulate them, and make life seem very dear to them, just before you let that peckerless Chink at them to kill them. You know everything there is to know about them . . . except what makes them tick."

"What do you mean?" she said. She threw back her arms in a langorous, feline stretch.

"Well," I said, "you don't know anything at all about me, for instance. You don't know or you wouldn't be trying any of your usual tricks on me at all. You don't seem to grasp that I'm on to your scam."

"Scam?"

"Yeah. You don't know I've got you pegged for what you are—a woman that hates and fears other women, even women who aren't as pretty as you, because they have something you haven't. And that's what makes you get into something as lousy as this white-slave thing."

"Have something I haven't?" she said. The voice was silken, dangerous. The eyes were cold as the outer planets. And now she turned that golden body to face me, offering herself to me. Those perfect, smooth, gently rounded breasts, their nipples hard and protruding; that smooth belly; that jutting mound of Venus with its triangle of sleek black hair. "Look, Carter. And remember. What woman

could have more to offer than I have?"

"Why, most of them have it, I'd guess. Even the homely ones and the dumpy ones and the wallflowers and the—but why explain? What they have is what you're missing. And you might call it humanity, and you might call it heart, but the place you'd go looking for it in them wouldn't be in their innards, up around chest-high. You'd go looking for it between their legs, and you wouldn't find it, because you wouldn't even know what it was that you were looking for."

"What do you mean?" she said. She spread those long slender legs, standing defiantly before me, the cleft of her body clearly visible at the bottom of her torso, the beringed toes of her bare feet splayed sensually.

"You've never had an orgasm in your life, have you? Not with men, not with women, not with dogs or horses or vibrators or whatever cute stuff you and that big Chink of yours can think up? No, I can see it in your eyes. I've hit the paydirt, haven't I? And you hate the men for enjoying you, and they have to pay because they couldn't make you enjoy them, so you have the Chink kill them, right? And you hate the women even more, because they're like you, and yet they have more than you can have, and they have to be punished for that, too, don't they? Punished by giving them the worst punishment a man-hater like you can imagine—which is to sell them into cribhouses where they have to satisfy men—nasty old men—again and again and again. . . ."

"Carter," she said, her voice husky again. "You could give me what I've missed all these years. I know it. At last I find a man worthy of myself, a

man who can take me past that level of sexual awareness that has always enchained me. You—you can show me." She advanced on me, her body lithe and beautiful, the gold on her shining in the firelight.

"Maybe I could," I said, getting painfully to my feet. "But I won't. Who the hell do you think you are? What makes you think I'd waste any time on the likes of you, knowing about you the way I do? You don't interest me at all. Go flash it at somebody else." I turned away from her—and just in time, too. I'd caught the flash of rage in her eye, and the almost imperceptible nod of the head. And now a hand the size of Primo Carnera's swished by my face, missing by no more than a hair.

I dived, rolled, putting space between him and me. And landed on my feet again, facing him, a fierce hatred burning in my guts. "Okay, Chiang," I said. "Come and get me, you big bastard."

TWENTY-FIVE

Now, however, I got a good look at him. And shook my head to clear the cobwebs away.

He was naked. Corpulently, grotesquely, obscenely naked. Naked as she was—and more so. Because down at his crotch, where prick and balls ought to be, there was nothing. Nothing but healed-over scar tissue where somebody had caponed him early in life. There must, I thought, be a peehole or something down there, but if so it wasn't visible.

Nothing.

I looked him in the eye now as we circled each other. His eye was as cold as hers, and as human. Well, fine and good. They were a pair. Marriage made in heaven. And in truth, if she *was* pair-bonded to anyone it was to this big voiceless, sexually denatured gorilla.

Out of the corner of my eye I could still see her, faintly; but she'd slunk off into the shadows, out of our way. Didn't want to miss a bit of it. And now

it came through to me that watching this—theoretically watching him kill me, for all that I had no intention of cooperating—would very likely be as close as she ever got to a real sexual turn-on. The only trigger that would come close to turning her on would be someone else's pain.

He attacked.

He was lightning-fast. His big broad foot lashed out in a karate kick. It was supposed to catch me in the middle of my chest and break some bones. I danced out of the way—and skipped back in to feint once at his gut, watch him pivot away, and kick him as hard as I could in the kidney.

It should have been a devastating blow. The kind that makes you bend over and piss blood for a week. Instead, all it did was anger him—and Chiang angry was a fearful sight. Imagine a fat version of The Incredible Hulk, bare-ass naked, with his dander up.

He came at me again, this time trying to grab me between those huge hands. I let him come—and then went down flat on my back to kick him in the gut with both feet—and send him sailing up over my head to crash on the floor behind me.

I was up in a second—but so was he. And this time he was so quick that I knew I wouldn't be able to get out of his way. There was only one thing to do, and I did it. It was the kind of thing Diego Puerta, or El Cordobes, might do to a charging bull.

I pulled out Hugo and stepped aside at the last possible moment. And, pivoting smartly, cut his throat with Hugo's seven inches of razor-sharp steel.

He went to his knees. His hands went to his

neck. He looked back around at me . . . and then down at the gouts of dark blood that poured from between his fingers. And slowly the life seemed to leave him, and he slid forward, and died. Silently; horribly silently. . . .

I looked around for her. But when I found her she had slipped back into that black cloak and those golden sandals. The hood of the cloak was pulled up over her head, and I couldn't see her face any more, much less that rich body. What I could see was the gun in her hand, and the red flash as she fired it at me point-blank. . . .

There was, for quite a time, a grey period in which bright lights kept coming on and people kept sticking pins in me and poking away at me. Faces kept bending over me, but I was too damn stoned on whatever it was that they kept pumping into me to really notice anything.

And the lights went on, and they went off, and the light and the dark kept alternating. . . .

. . . and then, suddenly as if nothing had happened, I awoke and there were faces around me, and they were familiar faces, and I wasn't zonked out any more and I hurt like merry hell, but all of a sudden I felt alive again.

And there was Mame Ferguson, as gorgeous as ever, looking down at me, that luscious face no more than a foot from mine, those wonderful boobs hanging down. . . . "Howdy, boss," she said.

"Well," I said in a voice too weak to be my own. "My faithful girl. You're looking fit."

"I hoped to hell you'd notice," she said. "I designed that bra myself. It's made out of parachute

cloth, and if *that* one hadn't got a rise out of you I'd have given you up for dead." Her smile was warm and loving. "Welcome back, Nick."

"Here," Angie said, and kissed me. Three times —no, four. Each time more delightfully than the last. "The first one was for me. The second one was for Traudl. She took a bullet in one arm back in the courtyard, and she's in a hospital in Zurich. The other two were for the two kids, and they'd have delivered the goods themselves if they hadn't had to get back to school." She winked. "Everything's dandy. Daddy doesn't suspect a thing. And the kids . . . well, they've had a little adventure. That's about it."

"Everything wrapped up?" I said. Damn that weak voice. "Hell. Including me. When can I get out of this damn bed?"

"Give it another week," Mame said. "You'll be okay. Hell, you'll be back to handball in a month. You. . . ."

"Lotus, God damn it," I said. "Did you get *her?*"

"Nope," Angie said. "She got away. But I'm gonna make that little cookie a special project of mine one of these days. Meanwhile, the slave ring is broken up. And Pivot is powerless."

"And AXE is back in business," Mame said. "Welcome back to the world, Nicky. Good to have you."

"Hey," I said. "I feel great. I'm hungry as hell. Who wants to go get me a coffee and Danish?"

"Me," said Mame. "So Gloria Steinem gets mad. Screw her. If a gal can't gofer every once and a goddam while, what's she good for?" She didn't want for an answer. *She* gave me a kiss now, and it

sent my head reeling. I didn't even see her leave.

"Angie," I said. "Wow, is everything working out nice. I must be doing something right."

She grinned down at me. "These guys think you're sick. Me, I bribed the doc—don't ask me how, a lady has to have a *few* secrets—to let me know how sick you were. He told me you were great, just as long as you stayed flat. Well, I can think of plenty of ways to keep you occupied without disobeying *that* order." She reached up and started unbuttoning her shirt.

"Hmm," I said appreciatively. "And the nurse? And the attendants? And all the people that come and go in the ward?"

"I'll bribe them one at a time," she said, pulling the shirt off. She wasn't wearing anything under it. "Don't ask me how. And as for whether you must be doing something right these days. . . ." She grinned down at me. Her hands were occupied with something out of sight, as though she were stepping out of something. "Well, don't worry about that. When you start doing it wrong I'll let you know about it."

"Is there a way of doing it wrong?" I asked, looking up at her as she crawled, all pink and cute and naked, into the big hospital bed.

"I don't know," she said, climbing on top of me, leaning down for a kiss even more luscious than before. "We'll go through the manual and rate them, Escoffier and *Guide Michelin* style. Now, for the antipasto course. . . ."

What can I say? It was a three-star afternoon. That's all.